A SUMMER
SENTENCE

A SUMMER SENTENCE

•

Carolynn Carey

AVALON BOOKS
NEW YORK

PRINTED IN THE UNITED STATES OF AMERICA
ON ACID-FREE PAPER
BY HADDON CRAFTSMEN, BLOOMSBURG, PENNSYLVANIA

For Iris Lester, who indulged my love
of reading when I was a child.
Thanks, Mom, for that and so much more.

And for Floyd and Allison,
who have always believed in me.
For once, words fail me.

Writers frequently thank their families first, and with good reason. Mine never stopped believing in me, for which I will always be grateful. I must also thank the Smoky Mountain Romance Writers for their friendship and magnificent support. Their devotion to writing and to sharing their knowledge has taught me so much. I will not name names because I would surely forget someone, but ladies, you know who you are. I also appreciate all the writers I have met during the years I have been a member of the Romance Writers of America. The late Carol Quinto was the first to offer me encouragement, and I know she would be thrilled for me now. Thank you, Carol. You are not forgotten.

Chapter One

"I can explain everything, Sheriff, really I can."
Megan Amelia Marsh drew a deep breath, tilted
her head back, and forced herself to meet Sheriff
Daniel McCray's gaze. His eyes were an astonish-
ing shade of topaz, but they were also narrowed in
disbelief. Megan pressed her right hand hard
against her belly. This was no time for a jittery
stomach, not when she'd been hauled into this
concrete block building that, like Mayberry,
appeared to house both the jail and the sheriff's
office. Being a stranger here, she figured she'd
better keep her wits about her long enough to convince this Tennessee lawman that she hadn't
intended to strike his deputy.

The sheriff raised his eyebrows and shot Megan

1

a smile that bordered on being a sneer. "Most folks can explain their actions, ma'am, but not always to my satisfaction. There's blood on Deputy Barnhart's face and that alone tells me a lot. So I'll listen to his account first, if you don't mind."

Megan nodded and lowered her gaze. No sense in letting the sheriff read the growing anger she knew would be reflected in her eyes. Deputy Barnhart's version was going to be a lot different than hers, and she figured she knew which one of them the sheriff would believe.

"Okay, Horace," the sheriff continued, "why don't you tell me why you brought this lady in."

Megan watched the deputy from the corner of her eye. He stood just to her left, and she couldn't help noticing that his right hand rested on a holstered gun at his belt. He threw his shoulders back, pulled his belly in, and turned to glare at Megan before redirecting his attention to the sheriff.

"First off, she was driving reckless out on Highway One-fifty-two, swerving all over the road. Then after I pulled her over, she jumped out of her car and assaulted me."

Megan gritted her teeth while the deputy reached to gingerly run a finger across the raw spot on his face where her sapphire ring had scratched his cheek. She could feel disapproval emanating from the sheriff.

"Is she on anything?"

Megan jerked her gaze up at that question, but the sheriff's attention was fixed on his deputy.

"Not so I could tell. She hadn't been drinking I'm pretty sure. Drugs I don't know about."

"Did you search her car?"

"Didn't take the time. I just put her in the patrol car and brought her straight here. Why?"

"We haven't had a lot of drug runners coming through McCray County, considering it's on the way to nowhere, but she could have gotten lost. Wayne County's been having problems, what with the interstate running through there, and I suppose some of the traffic could be drifting over our way. What kind of car was she driving?"

"One of them expensive ones. A BMW, I think."

"You'd better go back and search the car—with the lady's permission, of course. We don't have a search warrant."

Megan met the sheriff's gaze. "You don't need a warrant." She lifted her chin. "I have nothing to hide."

The sheriff nodded before turning back to his deputy. "You have her permission, so go back and check out the car."

"All right. Want me to lock her up first?"

"No, you go ahead. I'll watch the prisoner."

The prisoner felt her knees turning to jelly and

quickly locked them. Reckless driving, assaulting an officer, and suspicion of running drugs. All in a county that was on the way to nowhere. Well, well, wasn't her luck holding today.

A screen door slammed as the deputy made his exit, and Megan realized she was now alone with the sheriff. His department must be a small one, she decided, seeing as there was no secretary or even a second deputy. In addition to the sheriff's desk, and one she assumed belonged to Deputy Barnhart, the office consisted of two battered file cabinets leaning against the back wall and half a dozen chairs. All except the sheriff's executive chair were straight-backed. The sheriff pointed to one beside his desk that sported a tear clear across the vinyl-covered bottom. "Have a seat, miss. You might as well make yourself comfortable until Horace gets back."

Megan stood where she was. "Could I give you my version of what happened while we wait?"

"Nope. I want Horace to be present before you say anything. Now why don't you take a seat— unless you'd prefer waiting in a cell?"

Megan clamped her lips together and quickly sat down in the chair beside the sheriff's desk. He had been working on some papers when Horace escorted her into the office, but he had immediately stood and stepped around the desk to greet them face to face. Now he returned to his chair and pulled the papers back in front of him.

She watched him flip a page and begin reading. He was a nice looking man, she decided. She might even describe him as handsome, with his even features and square chin. His hair, a shade lighter than his tan uniform, appeared to be bleached a bit by the summer sun, and he wore it just above his collar. She wondered if he could feel her looking at him. If he did, he was ignoring her.

If only she could ignore the jagged rip in the seat of her chair. She had barely noticed the tear when she first sat down, but now she figured she knew what it felt like to sit on a row of crocodile teeth.

She shifted in her seat, then shifted again. It didn't help.

The next time she shifted, the chair seat shifted with her. Apparently it had been loose, merely resting on the square metal frame to which it had once been bolted. When the seat fell through the frame, Megan's rump followed.

She bit back a squeal of surprise but could do nothing to muffle the clatter of the chair seat when it hit the tile floor.

Nor could she move. Her behind was firmly lodged in the metal frame. She tried to free herself but couldn't get enough leverage. Her feet couldn't touch the floor, and the edges of the frame were too narrow to support her efforts to push herself up.

The sheriff's eyebrows shot up and his lips twitched. "In a bind, are you, Miss Marsh?"

Megan swallowed the sharp retort she longed to make. "You could say that," she murmured. She could feel blood rushing to her face, not to mention her derriere.

The sheriff stood, stepped to the side of the desk, and offered Megan his hand.

She reached up to him and was strangely comforted when his hand, large and warm, closed around hers.

He tugged gently. Nothing happened.

He tugged again. And then again, harder. Megan's rump didn't budge.

"You're really wedged in there," the sheriff noted.

Megan had thought her face couldn't grow any warmer. She had been wrong.

The sheriff stepped back and tilted his head to one side, apparently studying the situation.

Megan wasn't sure, but she thought her legs were going numb. "Perhaps if you tilted the chair forward until my feet are on the floor, I could free myself."

The sheriff's quick frown suggested he was skeptical, but after a second of thought, he shrugged. "We'll give it a try." He stepped around to the back of the chair and gently tilted it forward.

"Stop! Stop!" The instant Megan's feet touched the floor, she knew this had not been a good idea. With her body bent forward, she was far too much off balance to deal with the chair stuck to her bottom.

"Don't panic, Miss Marsh. I won't let you fall."

Megan realized the only reason she hadn't toppled over was because the sheriff still held onto the chair. Her mind raced. "Maybe if you ease me forward until the palms of my hands rest on the floor, you can pull the chair off of me."

"It's worth a try." The sheriff slowly tilted Megan forward. "Here you go."

Megan had never imagined she could feel so ridiculous. Here she was, bent over double with her hands and feet on the floor, her rump stuck up in the air, and a chair firmly attached to her posterior.

"I'll just tug on the chair legs here."

Megan felt the tug but she didn't feel the chair loosen.

"That thing's really stuck," the sheriff said, an unnecessary observation in Megan's opinion, but she didn't feel she was in any position to complain. She swallowed her irritation and said nothing.

The sheriff cleared his throat. "Excuse me, Miss Marsh, but I'm going to have to prop my knee against your, ah, your rear portion here, in order to get enough leverage to pull the chair off. With your permission, of course."

Megan stifled a whimper. "Permission granted."

The sheriff's knee pushed against Megan's bottom for less than ten seconds before the chair released her. She toppled forward, landing belly first on the floor. The sheriff dropped the chair and fell to his knees beside her. "Miss Marsh? Are you all right?"

Megan wanted to cry. She wanted to cry and to scream and to bang her fists against the tile floor. But she did none of those things. "I'm fine, thank you, Sheriff McCray," she said with as much dignity as she could muster.

"Here, let me help you up."

Now that she could move on her own, Megan would have preferred to get up by herself, but the sheriff had already slipped one hand beneath her arm and she didn't want to appear unappreciative. She allowed him to help her stand.

"Maybe you'd better sit in that chair over there."

Megan glanced at the chair the sheriff had indicated. Except for boasting a smaller rip, it looked identical to the one that had recently attached itself to her behind. "I'll stand for a while if I may."

"Suit yourself."

*   *   *

Daniel sat back down in his desk chair. He straightened the pile of papers in front of him and pretended to read the blank incident report on top of the stack. Miss Marsh's presence had unnerved him from the second Horace escorted her though the front door.

First of all, she was one of those females who looked as though they spent their entire lives learning how to look perfect, even in simple slacks and a blouse.

She had money, that much was obvious. Daniel had been exposed to his ex-fiancee's expensive tastes enough to recognize that Miss Marsh's simple navy slacks probably cost more than his weekly pay, and her plain blue blouse was definitely silk.

Even her hair looked expensive. If that dark chestnut color wasn't natural, it has been produced at one of those really fancy salons. Which probably explained how hair could look even silkier than silk. And the cut was fantastic too. Daniel had always admired that blunt cut that swung when a female moved her head.

In other words, Miss Marsh was the opposite of the type of female Daniel hoped to find someday. What he needed was a local girl, someone who had been born in McCray County. Preferably the girl of his dreams would have grown up in a large extended family like his own, and her family tree would be as deeply rooted in the soil of McCray County as his. She would understand and support his belief in the need for continuity from generation to generation.

Kaitlin had taught him what he needed in a woman when she returned his ring and announced she was dumping him and McCray County for a chance to make it big in Hollywood. She had also taught him that he did not need a pretty female with too much money and too little sense of community.

Unfortunately, despite knowing what he didn't need, Daniel couldn't keep his gaze from wandering back to Miss Marsh. She had drifted over to the bulletin board and now studied the posters there as though she hoped to memorize the features of each of the FBI's Ten Most Wanted.

Daniel suspected she was really trying to keep from facing him. He had noticed her blushes and regretted that she had been embarrassed. The fact that she blushed so readily surprised him. Most girls of her station, he would have thought, would be more worldly than that.

And she should be quite sophisticated, considering the money that must be at her disposal. She even smelled expensive. Her perfume exuded a clean fragrance, not at all heavy, but it possessed a seductive quality that Daniel had never experienced before.

He wished Horace would hurry back. He needed to hear that there was nothing illegal in that car. Then he would listen to this young woman's story, whatever it might be, and hopefully let her go. She couldn't get out of town fast enough to suit him.

Megan couldn't help noting, out of the corner of her eye, that the sheriff kept glancing her way. Based on his scowl, she figured he expected her to make a break for the front door at any minute. Moving slowly and trying to project an aura of innocence, she strolled over to the side window and stared through the dusty blinds at an asphalt parking lot. It was still early in June, but already waves of heat rose from the blacktop. The summer promised to be a hot one. Megan hoped she didn't spend it locked in a cell in Sheriff McCray's jail in what appeared to be his county. The McCrays must go back a long way to have the county named after them. That meant their influence would be substantial.

Tears pooled in Megan's eyes, but she blinked them away. She refused to cry, even if she did have a right to feel sorry for herself. Learning about her father's actions had shaken her to her very core, and now, when she had finally decided to strike out on her own to pursue her dream, she had landed in trouble the very first thing. Well, she wouldn't be calling her father, even if she ended up *under* the jail in McCray County.

No. She wasn't going to fall back into her old pattern of letting her family fix everything. She would get out of this herself, somehow or another. She only hoped—

Oh dear! Deputy Barnhart had just pulled into the parking lot. Megan's stomach turned a half flip while she watched the deputy get out of the car and head toward the office.

She hurried to the sheriff's desk. She preferred to be near him when Deputy Barnhart entered. "He's back," she said, then turned toward the front door. She felt immensely comforted when the sheriff stood and walked around the desk to stand beside her.

Deputy Barnhart hurried into the office carrying a small brown paper bag in his right hand. He stood before the sheriff and Megan, then pulled a bottle from the bag. It was half full of a light brown liquid.

"I found this stuffed under the passenger's seat," he said, waving the bottle in front of Megan's face. "Guess this Tennessee sour mash whiskey might enter into how bad you was driving, Miss Marsh."

Chapter Two

Megan's eyes widened in horror. She took a quick step backward, away from the deputy and that half-empty bottle, and her right heel landed on the sheriff's booted toe. She stumbled, and he quickly wrapped an arm around her waist. She allowed herself to lean back against his chest for a split second, to absorb the warmth of his body and inhale the faint lemony fragrance of his after-shave. Then she straightened and stepped away from his steadying arm. "I've never seen that bottle before in my life," she said.

Horace snorted. "That's what everybody says."

Megan glanced at the sheriff and saw him roll his eyes toward the ceiling, almost as though he, too, wished Horace was not so happy with his

13

find. But he quickly lowered his gaze, frowned, and addressed Megan in a stern tone. "If the whiskey isn't yours, Miss Marsh, where did it come from?"

Megan frowned. "I don't know." Her brow suddenly cleared. "Jason—Jason must have left it in my car."

Horace snorted again. "I wouldn't doubt you run drugs for this Jason. There's a lot of that going on around these parts. Who is this Jason feller anyway?"

Megan decided her wisest course was to ignore Horace. She turned to the sheriff. "Jason is my cousin. He's a freshman in college, and I loaned him my car last weekend. He was taking a girl to a party, and he wanted to make a good impression."

"Does your cousin figure drinking expensive whiskey is the way to impress a girl?"

"I wouldn't have thought so, but obviously I don't know Jason as well as I thought I did." Megan clenched her teeth and blew her breath out in a long sigh. If she ever got out of jail, she would see to it that Jason's father grounded him for at least the next forty years.

Daniel nodded slowly. He was perfectly willing to accept Miss Marsh's word for the duplicity of her cousin. He just hoped Horace didn't object too strenuously. The deputy, he knew, would be thrilled to toss Miss Marsh into jail. Horace already thought Daniel coddled the few lawbreakers they encountered in McCray County.

"Well, Miss Marsh," Daniel began, "I am willing to accept that you—" He paused when the little bell over the front door jingled. He turned to see who their visitor was, then suppressed a groan.

Horace grinned broadly. "Good morning, Judge."

The man who strode into the room was tall and broad-shouldered with a head of white hair that contrasted handsomely with his tanned face. A wide smile showcased his even white teeth and brightened his blue-green eyes.

"Hello, Horace." The newcomer's voice was deep and his tone jovial. "How are you this fine day?"

Horace threw his shoulders back and his chest out. "Had a busy morning, Judge. Got us a prisoner here. I found half a bottle of whiskey in her car just a few minutes ago. Before that she assaulted me after I pulled her over for reckless driving."

The judge looked at Megan with raised eyebrows. "Quite the desperado, aren't you, ma'am?" he said with an exaggerated wink, then turned to Daniel. "Good morning, Danny boy."

Daniel sighed. "Hello, Uncle Bob. What can I do for you?"

"I dropped by to invite you to the house for supper tonight. Your Aunt Evelyn said to tell you we're having pot roast. But seems like my timing might be fortuitous. Are you going to be needing a judge here pretty soon?"

"I'm not sure I'll be pressing charges."

"What?" Horace slapped a hand to his scratched cheek. "She assaulted me."

The judge frowned. "Sounds to me as though the lady has broken a few of our laws, Daniel. You can't just let that slide."

"She had an explanation for the whiskey," Daniel said.

"They all do," Horace interjected.

"What about the assault?" the judge inquired.

"I was just going to ask Miss Marsh for her side of the story." Between Horace and his Uncle Bob, Daniel felt as though he was on trial himself.

"I don't know why you want her side of the story," Horace objected. "I told you what happened."

"Yes, you did," Daniel said softly, trying to hide the fact that he was fast losing patience with his deputy. "But you may recall that the accused person in our society still has a right to a defense."

"True." The judge nodded his head vigorously. "Do you want me to call your Uncle Josh to come represent her?"

"She doesn't need an attorney yet, Uncle Bob. I

haven't even decided whether to charge her with anything."

"That doesn't mean she shouldn't have an attorney. Josh would probably tell her not to say a word to you. Have you advised her of her rights?"

"First I wanted to hear her side of the story in hope I could just let her go."

"Seems irregular to me," the judge said. "Why are you in such a hurry to let her go?" He looked at Megan and narrowed his eyes. "Pretty little thing, isn't she?" he murmured.

Daniel's jaw ached. It always did when he suppressed a strong desire to deck one of his uncles. They thought they had a right to help him live his life, and his Uncle Bob was the worst of the lot because, despite his good-old-boy mannerisms, he was the most intelligent of them all. If Daniel wasn't extremely careful, his Uncle Bob would figure out exactly why he wanted to hustle Miss Marsh out of town so quickly.

And his need to get rid of her increased by the minute. He didn't even have to be looking at her to feel the tug of her appeal. Something about her mere presence turned his mouth dry and heated his blood. He wished he had experienced an attraction one-tenth this strong for just one of the local women he had dated. He would have proposed on the spot.

Daniel became aware that while he was thinking about his attraction to Miss Marsh, his uncle had been talking to him. "I'm sorry, Uncle Bob. I didn't hear what you said."

The judge's eyes widened momentarily while a smile tugged at the corners of his lips. "I merely said that perhaps you're right. I don't believe the prisoner needs an attorney after all. Unless she insists, of course." He turned to Megan with his eyebrows raised. "Well, Miz Marsh, what do you say?"

Megan had listened with growing disbelief while the three men discussed her situation. Did they think she was a complete idiot? She knew she had a right to an attorney if she asked for one.

And she certainly didn't need to call on the sheriff's Uncle Josh for representation. She had three maternal uncles of her own who were in criminal law, not to mention her father and his two brothers who were in corporate law but would have rushed to her side had they known she was in trouble.

Thank goodness none of them knew.

Megan felt certain she could handle this situation herself if only the sheriff would refrain from advising her of her rights so she could tell her story without worrying that her words would be used against her. She had a feeling the sheriff wanted to let her go. Horace did not, of course, and she couldn't tell yet about the judge. She turned to the sheriff.

"I promise you, Sheriff McCray, that I didn't intentionally hit Deputy Barnhart. In fact, the only reason I was driving erratically in the first place was because a bee had gotten into the car when I rolled my window down and I kept having to duck to keep it from flying into my face. When Deputy Barnhart—"

The judge threw up a hand. "Why didn't you just pull off the highway, Miz Marsh?"

"The road was too narrow. I had spotted a wide shoulder ahead and was already slowing down so I could stop there when I heard Deputy Barnhart's siren."

"She did pull off right away," Horace allowed. "Maybe that's why I wasn't expecting any trouble out of her."

"And I certainly didn't intend to cause any trouble," Megan said. "In fact, I wouldn't have budged out of my seat if the bee had stayed away from me. But just as Deputy Barnhart walked up beside my car door, the bee flew into my hair. I panicked. I jumped out, accidentally bumping into Deputy Barnhart, and then I started waving my arms, trying to get that bee out of my hair. That's when I accidentally slapped the deputy, and my ring cut his face. I tried to explain to him about the bee, but I couldn't seem to make him understand."

"Sounds reasonable to me," the sheriff said quickly.

"Hogwash." Horace's jaw jutted out. "Pure hogwash. I never saw anything flying around her head."

The judge waved his hands in the air. "Now, now, gentlemen, there's no cause for dissension. After all, I'm the judge, and I say that the bee story is too unbelievable not to be the truth. But the open bottle of whiskey, now that's another kettle of fish." Deep furrows appeared on his forehead and he shook his head, as though mourning the downfall of an entire generation.

"There's no evidence she had been drinking," the sheriff said, eliciting a quick frown from Horace.

"I explained about the whiskey," Megan interjected.

"Well now, Miz Marsh." The judge regarded her with a solemn expression on his face. "As I said, I can buy the bee story, but I just can't overlook this open bottle business. I'm going to have to sentence you to four weeks of community service here in McCray County."

"Sentence her?" The sheriff gaped at his uncle. "Have you lost your mind? You can't sentence her. She hasn't had a trial. She hasn't even been charged with a crime."

"Well, Daniel, my boy, I suppose we *could* go to all that trouble, but it seems senseless to me."

"Senseless? Uncle Bob, you're a judge. You've got to be aware that we have laws in this country that have nothing to do with sense. No, wait. What I meant to say was—"

"Yes, yes, I know what you meant. But you really should consider charging the lady with something. Otherwise the mayor is going to be pretty distressed. He's been complaining about us not posting as many arrests as they're having over in Wayne County."

"I am not—I repeat *not*—arresting people just so you and the mayor can keep up with the county next door."

"And," Megan interjected, "I am *not* guilty of breaking any laws."

The judge turned to her with a smile that reminded her of her father when he wasn't believing a word she said. "But that opened bottle of whiskey was in your car, wasn't it, Miz Marsh?"

"Well, yes, but—"

"Then it was in your possession, lock, stock, and bottle." He chuckled merrily at his play on words.

"Very funny, Uncle Bob," the sheriff said through clenched teeth. "Now consider this. If Miss Marsh didn't actually put the partial bottle of whiskey in her vehicle, I think we could say she didn't really possess it."

"Sorry, Daniel, but I don't see it that way.

However, if Miz Marsh agrees to the four weeks of community service and stays out of trouble during that time, I'll see to it that her record is spotless when she drives off from here."

Megan had come to the realization that the judge was more interested in her doing community service than in charging her with a crime. She didn't understand why, but the community service seemed extremely important to him. Of course the whole thing was highly irregular, and she could have placed one phone call and summoned half a dozen high profile attorneys to her side, but she was beginning to think the judge's plan had merit.

After all, she had wanted to get away from Atlanta and her father for a while, and if she could handle this situation on her own, she would prove both to her father and, more importantly, to herself that she could handle her chosen profession.

"I accept the sentence," she said.

The sheriff looked at her with eyes that appeared to be glazing over. "You're pleading innocent and, at the same time, accepting a sentence for the crime you say you didn't commit?"

"That's correct."

"You're as crazy as these two." He waved an arm to encompass both his deputy and his uncle.

"In that case, she should fit in perfectly around here," the judge said. He draped an arm around Megan's shoulder. "We'll walk down to Sonny's

Diner for lunch, Miz Marsh, and I'll introduce you to some of the people you'll be getting to know during the next four weeks."

"Excuse me, Uncle Bob." The sheriff's tone was heavy with sarcasm. "Before you and the prisoner depart for the diner for lunch and introductions, could you share with me exactly what work you intend for Miss Marsh to do to fulfill her community service obligation?"

"I thought I'd let you determine that, my boy."

"Oh no. You sentenced her. You have to define the sentence."

The judge shrugged. "Miz Marsh and I will talk about that over lunch. I'm sure between the two of us, we'll come up with some ideas. But if I determine the type of community service she has to do, you'll be responsible for monitoring her. That's the law."

"Uncle Bob, sometimes I don't think you'd recognize the law if it walked up and bit you on the—"

"Now, now, Daniel. No need to get riled. I'll bring Miz Marsh back after lunch and we'll all have a nice discussion and map out the next four weeks."

The sheriff marched over to a rack beside the front door and jerked his hat off a hook. "While you're taking Miss Marsh to lunch, I'll start working on some of the details you appear to be ignoring, such as where the devil she's going to stay while she's in town."

"I won't be in jail then?" Megan asked.

The sheriff pulled in a deep breath. "I can't put you in jail, Miss Marsh," he said, exhaling through his teeth. "You haven't been charged with a crime. You haven't been tried for a crime. You haven't been convicted of a crime. You've only been sentenced for a crime."

"Well, we wouldn't want Miz Marsh staying in jail, anyway. She's been kind enough to accept her sentence and save us the cost of a trial. Surely the county could put her up at the bed and breakfast."

Daniel glared at his uncle. "Not out of the sheriff's budget, it couldn't. I thought I'd ask Dorothy Crabtree if she has any vacant rooms in her boardinghouse."

The judge beamed. "I knew we could count on you to come up with some ideas, my boy." He turned to Megan and offered his arm. "Now don't you worry, Miz Marsh. We'll make sure this community service sentence isn't one bit unpleasant for you."

"In fact," he muttered under his breath while turning to wave good-bye to Horace, "if I'm half the schemer I think I am, it'll be so pleasant you'll want to turn it into a life sentence."

Chapter Three

"Well, Miz Marsh, what do you think of our town's most prominent street?" Judge McCray paused under one of the mature maples shading Kessler Boulevard and flung his arms wide to encompass the street's structures—two Victorians, half a dozen unpretentious two-story houses, three bungalows set amongst lilac bushes and dogwoods, and two stone houses with discreet business signs in their front yards.

"It's charming," Megan said. She wasn't just being polite. There was a cozy sense of friendliness about the quiet street that appealed to her, much different from the gated community where she had always lived.

The judge pointed to the stone building on the right. "Josh's law offices are on the first floor of that house and he lives upstairs. The house next door has been converted to offices for my brother Richard's architectural firm. He built himself a house on the lake."

"How many brothers do you have?"

"Just those two plus Daniel's father, Bill."

"And what does he do?"

"He does a little farming, and he's also mayor of our county seat, Barbourville. We're inside the city limits now. Daniel is the sheriff of McCray County, but he also handles law enforcement for Barbourville. The town's too small for its own police department."

"Mayor?" Megan said, latching onto the word that had captured her attention. "The sheriff's father is the mayor?"

"Yes, but don't you be thinking that the county's run by McCrays, Miz Marsh. We just take our civic duties seriously, that's all. Now let's get on down to the diner before Sonny's daily special is all gone." He offered his arm again, and the two continued down Kessler Boulevard.

As they approached the center of town, traffic picked up and the buildings grew larger. They passed Moser's Memorial Library, the Wayne Hardware Store, Gwen's Paints and Things, and the McCray County Courthouse before stopping at the unpretentious front door of Sonny's Diner.

Megan's stomach knotted up. She had no idea what the judge was going to tell the people inside, and while she knew the rules of etiquette for most situations, she sure didn't know what she would say to folks who had just been told she was the town's newest felon.

"Now don't you worry, Miz Marsh." The judge turned to Megan with a smile. "I don't plan to lie to anybody, but I've got no qualms about omitting a few details. We'll just say you're going to be visiting the town for a while, which is certainly true. Then, after we figure out what your community service will be, we'll explain that you wanted to be of use to the townsfolk. True, every word of it!"

Megan's stomach settled down a bit. "Thank you, Judge McCray."

He grinned, patted her on the hand, and opened the door for her.

When she stepped inside the diner, Megan felt as though she had stepped back in time fifty years. Sonny's Diner possessed the yesteryear charm that dozens of diners in Atlanta had spent thousands of dollars trying to replicate.

But she had little time to admire the marble counter or the antique jukebox. Almost every booth and table was occupied, and the judge led her from one to another, introducing her to at least a dozen people, all of whom greeted her cordially. If anyone noticed that the judge was vague about Megan's purpose in visiting Barbourville, no one was so rude as to press for more details.

One of the first people Megan met was the sheriff's father, Mayor Bill McCray. All of the McCray men appeared to possess those appealing blue-green eyes, Megan noticed, although Bill McCray's weren't nearly as mesmerizing as his son's. Nor was Mayor McCray as tall as the sheriff, but both had the same upward tilt to their lips that made them appear always to be on the verge of a smile.

The mayor welcomed Megan to Barbourville and then begged permission to introduce her to his wife, Martha Barbour McCray.

Megan was too steeped in the intricacies of society to overlook the significance of the mayor including his wife's maiden name in his introduction. Obviously the Barbours, like the McCrays, were an old family in this region, which meant the sheriff was well connected on both sides of his family.

Megan watched Martha McCray's gaze flicker over her, from her Oscar de la Renta blouse and slacks to her Chanel handbag to her Gucci loafers. Mrs. McCray's eyes widened briefly. Her smile was polite but reserved. "Welcome to

Barbourville, Miss Marsh. Will you be making a long stay with us?"

"Miz Marsh is going to be helping us out a little around here, Martha. I'll explain tonight over supper. You and Bill are invited. Evelyn's fixing pot roast." He looked toward the back of the restaurant. "I see Josh and Richard in their usual booth. I want to introduce Miz Marsh to the attorney and architect in the family."

By the time the judge finished his introductions, Megan had reached two conclusions. First, at least half these people were related to each other, either through blood or through marriage.

Second, she would never fit in unless she came up with a different wardrobe. Although her navy slacks and blue blouse would be considered understated in her usual milieu, they were out of place in Barbourville. Even worse, the clothes she had packed last night were more suited to an expensive spa than to a sentence of community service.

"Is there a clothing store around here?" she asked the judge.

"There's Beth Ann Stanfield's place next door, but you haven't had lunch yet. You can shop after you eat."

"I'm really not hungry, sir. If you don't mind, I'll leave you to your lunch, and I'll meet you back here as soon as I've had a chance to replenish my wardrobe."

The judge smiled and nodded. "I know, I know. You ladies would rather shop than eat. Well, I guess I can't complain when the outcome is so attractive. Take your time. I'll be here when you finish."

Megan flashed him a smile and hurried out of the diner.

Beth Ann's clothing store was located just a few steps from the restaurant. The display window had been decorated in a theme suited for the upcoming summer, with a mannequin dressed in blue jean shorts and a halter top and seated on a lawn chair surrounded by beach balls. Megan was inclined to think she could find just what she needed inside.

The store was empty of customers, but an attractive young woman stood behind a wooden counter. Her smile of welcome flickered when she saw that Megan wasn't one of her regulars. She quickly stuffed a half-eaten hamburger under the counter and wiped her fingers on a paper napkin. "Good afternoon. I'm Beth Ann. Can I help you?"

Megan couldn't help feeling a tad jealous of the woman's curly red hair, green eyes, and porcelain skin. But she was also drawn to Beth Ann's direct gaze and genuine smile.

"I need a complete wardrobe," Megan said.

Beth Ann's eyes widened. "Complete? What do you mean, complete?"

"I need everything—blue jeans, shorts, shirts, shoes, socks, a skirt or two. Can you help me?"

Beth Ann's face split into a wide grin. "I sure can. What do you want to start with?"

Megan looked around. The shop was quite different from the upscale stores she usually patronized. Here there were no slick salesclerks, broad aisles, or bright lighting. Instead, crowded racks of clothing took up most of the floor space, and special items were displayed on their hangers, which were hooked over nails driven into the dark paneled walls.

Megan pointed high on the wall to a knit top with horizontal stripes of tomato red, lime green, and lemon yellow. "That's a nice shirt. Do you have any shorts to go with it?"

"It's part of a group of coordinates, so I have shorts in all three shades. Which do you prefer?"

"Mmmm. I'll take all three, along with that plaid cotton blouse that also seems to coordinate with everything."

Beth Ann's grin widened. "I like you, lady."

Megan grinned back. "The name's Megan. And I like you too."

By the time she had selected outfits that would work for any situation she could imagine arising during her community service, Megan had created a stack two-feet high on Beth Ann's countertop.

Thank goodness she had stopped at the bank on her way out of Atlanta. While she usually didn't carry around $4,000 in cash, she was glad she had indulged her impulse to withdraw plenty of money.

Beth Ann finished ringing up Megan's selections, then stared with widened eyes at the figure on her cash register. "Will that be all?" Her voice was not quite steady.

"For today at least. What's the damage?"

Beth Ann had to clear her throat twice before she could voice the total.

Megan reached into her purse and pulled out a bank envelope. She counted out eleven $100 bills and handed them across the counter, then dropped the bills when she saw tears rolling down Beth Ann's white cheeks. "What's wrong, Beth Ann? Is it something I said? Have I depleted your stock too much? Whatever I've done, I'm sorry, and I'll return anything you want me to. I didn't mean to upset you."

Beth Ann's tears turned into sobs. "I'm not upset, Megan. I'm happy. Sales have been horrible lately. In fact, I haven't sold this much in the last month altogether. And it's been so worrisome because Trevor—he's my son—wants the same things other kids have and I have to tell him 'No' so often. And now the school is saying he needs special tutoring in reading this summer to keep from being held back next year and I just don't have the money to hire anybody."

Beth Ann's white cheeks slowly leached into red. "Oh! I'm so sorry! I have no right to complain about all my problems when you've been so nice."

"Nonsense." Megan stepped around the counter and enveloped Beth Ann in a hug. "It sounds as though you're having more than your share of problems right now."

Beth Ann returned Megan's hug but then stepped back and lifted her chin. "It's true I've had more expenses than usual lately, but I'll manage," she said, then sighed. "If only I hadn't inherited that white elephant of a house, I wouldn't have so many repairs to pay for, but I guess I'd be paying about as much in rent." Her smile appeared forced. "Thanks, Megan. I appreciate your kindness. If there's ever anything I can do for you . . ."

Megan leaned against the counter. "Maybe there is. Do you have an extra bedroom in this white elephant of a house of yours?"

"I've got half a dozen extra bedrooms. My Great Aunt Brenda left the house to me, and it was built back in the days when folks had a dozen kids or more."

"Would you consider renting me a room for the next four weeks? I really need a place to stay."

"Are you sure you don't want some place fancier, like the bed and breakfast south of town?"

"No, I'd much prefer to stay with you." Megan paused, not sure how to pose the question she needed to ask. She had already noticed that Beth Ann wore no wedding ring, but that didn't mean she lived alone. "Unless," she continued, "maybe someone else living in the house wouldn't want you to rent out a room."

Beth Ann shook her head. "There's just me and Trevor. Trevor's daddy was killed in a car accident before Trevor was born. Jim and I had only been married six months. Things were rough for a while. That's why Great Aunt Brenda left me her house. She thought she was helping."

"I'm sorry."

"Thanks. We're doing better now. Most of the time at least. But you really are welcome to rent a room from me. I would love having the company."

"Great. Where's your house located?"

"Two blocks from here. It was one of the first houses built on the east side of town."

"That sounds fine. I'll pay in advance. And Beth Ann . . ."

"Yes?"

"This is just a suggestion, but seeing as I have a college degree in education with a concentration in reading, I'd be delighted to work with Trevor to improve his reading skills. Just informally, you understand."

Beth Ann's eyes widened. "Megan, it's almost like you're an answer to my prayers."

Megan turned solemn. "Beth Ann, if I'm going to be moving into your house and teaching your son, there's something you have a right to know. Let me tell you what happened to me last night and this morning."

Five minutes later, Beth Ann's howls of laughter had diminished into a few gurgles of mirth. "I'm sorry, Megan. I know this isn't funny to you, but I would have loved to hear old Horace Barnhart whining about a little scratch on his cheek. And poor Daniel. We were in high school together, so I know that his uncles have always driven him crazy, with Judge McCray being the worst of the lot."

"But you believe me about my erratic driving and the whiskey under my passenger's seat?"

"Absolutely, but I do need to ask you a personal question."

"Anything."

"Where did you get all of that money?"

Megan didn't hesitate. "I inherited it."

"Inherited?"

"Yes, from my mother's side of the family. She died when I was eight. She had inherited a substantial sum of money from a maternal aunt and, since I was an only child, the trust fund came to me. I've never touched the principal because my father felt it was his responsibility to support and educate me. But occasionally, when I really want to splurge on something, I dip into the interest. That's what I did this morning."

"Because of what happened between you and your father last night?"

"Yes." Megan sighed. "I know I sound imma-ture, and if you don't want me in your—"

"Hush, now," Beth Ann interrupted. "I'll be delighted to have you in my home. I'd close the shop up for a while and help you get settled right now, but you have to go back and meet the judge, don't you?"

"I'm afraid so. And Beth Ann, frankly, I'm a lit-tle puzzled. Why would he have insisted on me doing community service when he can't even think of anything for me to do?"

"Now don't you worry, Meg. May I call you Meg?"

Megan thought for a second. No one had ever called her Meg but she rather liked it. "Sure, just between us friends."

"Great. Now, Meg, don't you worry about the judge. He can be a little weird at times, probably because he's so smart, but there isn't a lecherous bone in his body. He won't do you any harm. We just need to come up with some community ser-vice for you to do."

"I figured I'd be picking up trash alongside the highway or something like that." Megan suppressed a shudder.

"You haven't done anything to warrant that kind of punishment. Wait! I know what you can do. You can teach."

"Teach? But it's summer, Beth Ann, and besides, while I have certification to teach in Georgia, I'm not certified in Tennessee."

"It wouldn't be anything formal, but I know half a dozen kids besides Trevor who've been having trouble with reading. You could set up a daily tutoring session for them in my parlor. It's big enough for a small school anyway."

Megan gaped. "You would do that for me, Beth Ann?"

"You'd be the one doing the favor, Meg, and it would be for the whole town. Everybody's interested in the kids doing well in school, but their English teacher is within a year of retiring and Mrs. Moulton just doesn't seem to be able to reach the students anymore."

"Your plan sounds wonderful, but do you think Judge McCray will agree?"

Beth Ann grinned. "He'll be purely delighted he doesn't have to come up with something on his own. And Daniel, who's probably worried that he's going to have to deal with another one of his uncle's harebrained schemes, is really going to be relieved. Come on, let's go see if we can locate them. I can't wait to see their faces when we tell them we have a plan."

Chapter Four

Daniel approached Sonny's Diner in one of the foulest moods he had experienced in years. Today had been a study in pure frustration.

First Horace had overreacted to a relatively minor traffic incident, bringing in that poor girl when he should have listened to her story and then let her go on her way.

Then his Uncle Bob had decided to turn the rules of law upside down.

Finally, he had spent the last hour unsuccessfully attempting to locate some place to house their uncharged felon. He had even checked with the bed and breakfast south of town, having decided he would pay Miss Marsh's bill out of his own pocket, but the B&B had been booked solid through the next month. After all, as the owner had pointed out, June was the beginning of the exodus of city people to the country. Nobody in the county would have any unoccupied rooms.

When Daniel pushed open the door of the diner, he was more in the mood to chomp on nails than to dine on Sonny's special. His disposition didn't improve when the first sound he heard was his Uncle Bob's laughter bouncing off the walls. Nor was he pleased to discover his parents seated at a table with the judge, Miss Marsh, and Beth Ann Stanfield.

Worst of all was the ridiculous leap his heart gave when his gaze lit on Megan Marsh. Lord, but she was beautiful! Unfortunately, she was also everything he didn't want in a female. He set his teeth and approached the table.

"Hello, son." Martha McCray motioned to a vacant chair beside her. "Sit down. Beth Ann was just telling us how Horace is crying assault over a scratch from Meg's ring."

Meg! Darn it all, he had left Miss Marsh and his uncle alone for a mere hour, and his own mother was already calling their pseudo prisoner Meg.

"Good news, Daniel my boy." The judge shot him a triumphant grin. "We've found Miz Marsh a place to stay, and we've made a determination about the community service she'll be fulfilling. That should make you happy."

Daniel dropped into the chair beside his mother and signaled the waitress for a cup of coffee. He had a feeling he would need something considerably stronger by the time he'd been apprised of his uncle's plans.

But it was his old high school friend, Beth Ann, who spoke up first. Her eyes sparkled. "Meg's going to be staying in one of my extra bedrooms, Daniel, and for her community service she's going to be running tutoring sessions in my parlor for some of the kids who've been having trouble with reading."

"Reading?" He turned to Megan and ruthlessly suppressed the surge of desire that immediately engulfed him. "What credentials do you have to teach reading, Miss Marsh?"

"A bachelor's degree in education with a concentration in reading," Megan replied with a tiny lift of her chin.

"I assume you can prove this claim."

Daniel didn't need Beth Ann's soft gasp or his mother's tightened lips to realize that Miss Marsh had already endeared herself to some of the citizens of McCray County. But he couldn't afford to accept either her or her story at face value. He was the sheriff, after all, and he had been entrusted with the welfare of these people. Besides, this entire situation was unusual if not downright bizarre.

He had a fairly good idea what his uncle was up to, of course, but he was increasingly puzzled by Miss Marsh's motivations. Why would a woman from an apparent background of wealth agree so readily to a trumped-up sentence that would keep her stuck in a small town for four weeks, especially when she must realize that a single phone call to an attorney would almost certainly result in her freedom?

Instead, she appeared delighted at the prospect of spending half the summer in isolated McCray County. In fact, although others around the table were glaring at Daniel, the seemingly content Miss Marsh flashed him a devastating smile. "Unfortunately, Sheriff McCray, I don't carry my diploma around with me, but I can give you the name of my alma mater, and you can verify my claim with a simple phone call."

"I'll do that, Miss Marsh, the first thing tomorrow morning. In the meanwhile, we need to go back to my office. There's some paperwork we should take care of."

The judge immediately leaned forward. "What paperwork? I thought you weren't going to charge Miz Marsh."

"I'm not. But there's the matter of her BMW that's parked on the shoulder of the road out on Highway One-fifty-two. I plan to bring it in and impound it."

"Impound?" Daniel's mother said. "Is that necessary?"

Daniel straightened in his chair. The joys of being a small-town sheriff were many, but having one's every action scrutinized by family was not one of them. In fact, that aspect of the job could become downright irritating.

He looked into his mother's face. "Yes, the impoundment is necessary, Mom. An open bottle of whiskey was found in Miss Marsh's car, but that's not the reason I'm impounding it. I wouldn't have the legal right to impound it for that reason because I never charged Miss Marsh with breaking any laws. She was merely sentenced by our estimable judge." He shot his uncle a meaningful glance. "The reason I'm impounding the car is to keep it safe for the next four weeks. Besides, I refuse on principle to allow someone who has volunteered for a sentence of community service to perform that service while tooling around town in a car that cost more than most people in this county earn over a two-year period."

Daniel wasn't surprised by the instant silence that reigned around the table. His family members weren't accustomed to his becoming annoyed with them. Obviously no one was quite sure what to say with the exception of Miss Marsh, who immediately stood.

"The sheriff is absolutely correct," she said. "I

see no reason why I would need the car, and I would much prefer that it be impounded. I'll be happy to sign any papers necessary to take care of that. Shall we go, Sheriff McCray?"

Daniel pushed himself to his feet. He hated getting irritated with the people who loved him and who only meant well by their interminable meddling. But a man had to draw a line. He only wished he didn't feel guilty for doing so. "Thank you, Miss Marsh, for accepting my viewpoint so readily." He waved her ahead of him, then followed her through the front door. It hadn't quite closed behind them before the buzz of conversation, muted but with an underlying note of excitement, arose in the diner behind them.

When they arrived at the station a short time later, the office was deserted. Daniel found a note on his desk from Horace saying that he was making his afternoon rounds and wouldn't be back in the office until his shift started the next morning.

Daniel tossed the note into the wastebasket, then motioned toward the chair beside his desk. "Have a seat, Miss Marsh."

Megan stepped to the front of the chair and looked down at the seat. "Oh no you don't!"

"What?" Daniel frowned at her in confusion.

"That is the same chair that nearly devoured me earlier today. I'll stand if it's all the same to you."

Daniel's frown deepened. "I called Horace and

asked him to replace that chair. He must have forgotten. I'll try to find a safer seat if you want to sit down."

"Thanks, but I'll stand. Besides, I can't imagine this will take long."

"The paperwork itself won't take long, but when I call the Stubblefields to go retrieve your car, I plan to have them come by here before they take it to the impoundment lot. If there's any damage, I'll need to list it and have you initial the list. That's for your protection as well as for the protection of the Stubblefields. If anything happens to the vehicle while it's in their lot, their insurance will cover the damages."

"That's fine. Besides, I need to get my suitcase out of the trunk before they lock my car up."

Daniel cleared his throat. "Another thing, Miss Marsh."

"Yes?"

"I need to know what figure you and Beth Ann set for your rent so I can fill out the paperwork to get the county to reimburse Beth Ann."

"That's not necessary. I've already paid Beth Ann in advance."

Daniel was surprised by the sudden flash of anger that enveloped him. After all, common sense would have dictated that he accept Miss Marsh's gesture. There was little doubt she could afford it.

But nothing in his dealings with her had made any sense, and this situation was no different. He realized he was either going to have to pay for her lodging in McCray County or end up feeling like the biggest heel in the state. This emotion obviously resulted from the male's eternal need to provide for the female, but understanding the emotion didn't lessen its impact. His tone when he spoke again was sterner than he had intended.

"In that case, I'll just revise the paperwork to have you reimbursed instead of Beth Ann. But understand this, Miss Marsh. You are *not* performing community service for a crime you didn't commit, and then paying out of your own pocket for a place to stay."

Megan was so startled by the sheriff's sudden mood swing, she inadvertently took a quick step backwards. The back side of her knees hit the edge of the chair behind her, and she plopped down onto the ripped seat, which instantly clattered to the floor below her.

"Oh no." Megan groaned.

"Don't tell me . . . ?" Daniel stared down at her.

"I'm afraid so." Megan felt a flush heating her face, but this time it was caused by anger rather than embarrassment. "So help me, if I get out of this chair in one piece, I'm going to take a sledgehammer to it."

Daniel's lips twitched. "I'd be careful about

tossing around threats of violence, Miss Marsh, at least until you're out of the clutches of that voracious chair."

"Speaking of clutches, Sheriff, would you mind taking my hand and seeing if you can pull me straight out this time. I don't think I'm wedged in as tightly as before."

"We'll give it a try." Daniel grasped her hand and gave it a healthy yank.

She flew straight out of the chair and into his arms.

To Daniel, holding her seemed like the most natural thing in the world. He first wrapped his arms around her to steady her, but when she leaned into him, he knew he couldn't let go. He looked into her upturned face and understood for the first time in his life that eyes could ensnare a man and bring him to his knees.

And her lips. Her lips suddenly became the center of his universe, more tempting than anything he had ever known. He lowered his head. She tilted hers back. The invitation was there. All he had to do was accept. He didn't think he could have refused even if his life had been on the line.

He touched her lips with his own, lightly, needing to prove to himself that this was real, that it was not a mirage.

No, it definitely was not a mirage. The sensations were real. Too real. Too powerful. But wonderful. Wonderful beyond anything he had ever imagined. He told himself he should end that kiss immediately. He was going to do just that. He was going to . . .

Before he could pull away, she wrapped her arms around him and deepened the kiss. She tasted of coffee and peppermint, tangy and sweet. There was a warmth to her, and a softness that Daniel had never experienced before.

But the softness was deceptive and the warmth was a prelude to heat that flared suddenly. His dazed mind conjured up fireworks and shooting stars. A storm at sunrise. An eagle soaring on air currents far above the mountain peaks. Images of beauty and of danger and of unimaginable delight.

Daniel had never dreamed a kiss could take him to such heights. He felt as though he had been given a taste of an exquisite corner of paradise. As though he had come back to a home he had never known existed. He wanted nothing so much as to lose himself in the magic of that kiss and never experience reality again.

Megan ended it. Not that she wanted to. She felt as though she could have spent the next ten years in this man's arms and still have longed for more. But that was a thought that terrified her. She would be in McCray County for only four weeks, but she had an agenda here.

And even though Daniel's kiss had been the most powerful, the most enticing she had ever known, she couldn't afford to become sidetracked. So she had called upon her dwindling strength and pushed him away.

He responded immediately. He released her, stepped back, and looked directly into her eyes. "I'm sorry, Miss Marsh. I had no right to do that."

Megan sighed. This day was becoming more complicated by the moment. First that powerful kiss, now Daniel's hangdog attitude. He looked as though he would happily flog himself if it was physically possible. "Please don't apologize for kissing me. I was as much a participant as you."

"Even if you were, I had no right—"

"You had every right. You weren't forcing anything on me."

"Perhaps not, but you need to understand right up front that you're not my type."

"Oh really?" Megan felt her temper rising. "And do you always kiss women who aren't your type with that sort of fervor?"

The sheriff winced. "No, I don't. It's just that, well, I find you attractive, Miss Marsh. Very, very attractive. But I've always planned on marrying a local girl. I still do."

Megan squared her shoulder. "It was a kiss, Sheriff, not a marriage proposal. Now will you quit making a federal case out of it and finish up the paperwork?"

The sheriff's face turned a bit ruddy, but he met Megan's gaze squarely. "You can't deny there's an unusual degree of attraction between us. Or is that just on my part?"

"You know it isn't," Megan said, her anger fading. "But I have my own life goals, Sheriff, and they can't be accomplished in the country, so we'll both just have to ignore the attraction between us. I think we can do that if we simply avoid each other's company. Now can we please finish here and let me get back to Beth Ann's store? She's staying late so I can pick up my purchases and she can take me home with her."

Daniel turned and pulled open a drawer in one of the file cabinets. "I'll fill out an impoundment form immediately. But there's no reason for Beth Ann to stay in the store late. She can take your purchases home with her, and I'll drop you off at her house."

Megan hesitated. She hated to extend her time in the sheriff's company, but she didn't want Beth Ann to have to wait on her either. "I'll accept your offer if it won't take you out of your way too much."

The sheriff looked up from the form, his expression solemn. "Didn't Beth Ann tell you?"

"Tell me? Tell me what?" Megan braced for his

answer. She could tell by the wary expression on his face that she wasn't going to like what she was about to hear.

"I assumed Beth Ann had already explained that my house is directly across the street from hers. You and I are going to be close neighbors while you're in town, Miss Marsh."

Chapter Five

Another hour passed before the Stubblefields arrived with Megan's car. The first thing she did was retrieve her suitcase and overnight bag from the trunk. Then the papers had to be signed and the Stubblefield brothers spent ten minutes assuring Megan they would be careful with her vehicle. Finally they left, and Daniel quickly locked up the office, escorted Megan out to his car, and opened the passenger's door for her.

Megan climbed in, slumped down in the seat, and stretched her legs out as far as they would go. She moaned softly, then turned toward the driver's seat and watched Daniel scoot under the steering wheel. His gaze cut to her legs and appeared to measure their length before he caught himself and looked up with a sheepish smile. His face flushed a bit, and he fumbled a second with the ignition key, then looked over his shoulder and put the car in reverse. "Tired?" he asked.

Megan pushed herself up in the seat and sighed. "Very! Let me tell you, the lifestyle of a desperado is downright exhausting."

He glanced at her from the corner of his eye. "I've heard rumors to that effect." He backed up a few feet, then pulled out onto Kessler Boulevard. "I'm sorry everything took so long this afternoon."

"It wasn't your fault the Stubblefields were tied up when you called them. I'm just glad you phoned Beth Ann and told her not to wait in the store for me."

He turned left onto Lewis Lane. "Where were you headed this morning when Horace stopped you?"

Megan shifted a bit in her seat. She didn't want to discuss last night's disagreement with her father, and her job-hunting plans were too uncertain to mention. Fortunately, she could easily share what her immediate intentions had been when she crossed the Tennessee line. "My mother's family lives in the North and I was on my way to visit them."

"Is your mother originally from the North?"

"She was born and raised in Chicago but moved

to Atlanta when she married my father. She died when I was eight years old."

He shot her a quick glance. "I'm sorry."

"Thanks." Megan decided it was time to change the subject. "Are we getting close to Beth Ann's house?"

"Just one more turn." He cut onto Redbud Road. "And if I'm not mistaken, there's Beth Ann waiting for us now."

Megan looked to her right. Sure enough, Beth Ann, dressed in a bright yellow sundress with daisies embroidered on the bodice, stood on the sidewalk, bouncing up and down on the toes of her yellow sandals. She started waving with both hands when they turned onto Redbud.

Daniel pulled over to the curb, and Beth Ann motioned for him to roll down his window. "Where have you two been? Judge McCray called half an hour ago. Daniel, you didn't forget, I hope, that your Aunt Evelyn invited you to supper? Meg and I are invited also. Trevor can't go. He's spending the night with Michael Stevens. Hurry, Meg, you'll want to freshen up. Can we ride with you, Daniel? I'm running low on gas."

"You're more than welcome to ride with me, but I need to feed Eisenhower before we go. Give me a call when you're ready and I'll drive over."

Megan climbed out of the car, retrieved her luggage from the back seat, and allowed Beth Ann to lead her toward the deep front porch that wrapped around the side of a massive Victorian house set back from the street in a large lot nearly overgrown with old plantings.

"Nice house," she commented, picking her way along flagstones nearly obscured by tall grass.

"For an army. For two people, it's a bit much. I can't begin to take care of it all. But Great Aunt Brenda wanted me to have it, so what else could I do? She was dead and I couldn't give it back."

Megan grinned. "Good point."

"I don't mean any disrespect to Aunt Brenda. It's just that these old places are so huge. Look at poor old Daniel, stuck in that monstrosity across the street with only Eisenhower for company."

"Who is Eisenhower anyway?"

Beth Ann grimaced. "A cat. Spoiled to death and ugly as sin." She opened the front door and led Megan into a massive foyer with a stairway on the left and a hallway on the right. "Your bedroom is upstairs, the second door on the left. I've laid out one of the new slack sets for you to wear tonight. I pressed it a little bit for you. I hope you approve of my choice."

"I'm sure it will be fine. But why name a cat Eisenhower?"

Beth Ann grinned. "Daniel is from a family that loves dogs, but he always had other tastes. When he was a kid, he was forever begging for a kitten.

His father finally gave in on one condition. Daniel had to name his cats for US presidents, starting with George Washington. Daniel's father was of the opinion that cats are worthless creatures, and he declared the only way he could figure to get any good out of them was by giving them names that would force his son to memorize our presidents and the order in which they were elected."

"And he's already up to Eisenhower?"

"He's had a lot of cats in his time. He used to visit the pound every time his family went to Knoxville. His mother would come home with a new dress, and Daniel would come home with a stray cat. Pretty soon the folks around here learned where to drop off unwanted litters."

"What's he going to do when he runs out of presidents?"

"He's going to start on the vice presidents. After that I don't know. Maybe secretaries of state. Now hurry, honey. Miss Evelyn is a great cook, but she doesn't like to set back supper too many times."

Bob and Evelyn McCray lived ten miles out of town in the house everybody in their family called "the home place." It was a rambling affair that had started off as a six-room farmhouse and had fortunately endured generations of additions without losing its architectural integrity. That it was loved was evident in the signs of constant care—a new roof, fresh paint, and an updated kitchen/dining area where there was room for everyone to sit around a massive oak table.

All the McCrays had gathered for supper. Megan had already met most of them at the diner, and everyone greeted her with casual friendliness. Daniel's mother, who instructed Megan to call her Martha, was waiting near the front door and immediately led Megan to the kitchen to introduce her to Judge McCray's wife.

"Welcome, my dear Meg. Call me Miss Evelyn. Everyone does." Miss Evelyn finished pouring a bowl of green beans and then turned to give Megan her hand. "I may call you Meg, I hope. Yes? Wonderful. Martha's already told me all about you. You mustn't let my husband browbeat you. Bob's entirely too bossy for his own good sometimes." She handed the beans to Martha, who carried them over to the table where they joined a huge roast surrounded by bowls of mashed potatoes, creamed peas, cheese grits, a congealed salad, and rolls.

Miss Evelyn continued. "Bob wanted me to seat you beside Daniel tonight, but I told him the rest of us deserved a chance to get to know you so you'll be seated on my right."

Supper was a noisy but cheerful affair. All four McCray brothers were there. Josh had brought his long-time lady friend, Lily Martin, the town librarian, and Richard was accompanied by his business partner, Eloise Smithfield. Beth Ann had been seated next to the mayor, and the judge occupied a chair at the far end of the table.

Miss Evelyn, as it turned out, considered herself the unofficial county historian. Her own ancestors, the Mosers, had settled in the area only a few years after the Barbours and McCrays, and Miss Evelyn knew as much about those families as she did her own.

"I noticed the Moser Memorial Library," Megan commented. "Is Kessler Boulevard named after an early county family too?"

"Yes, dear, but unfortunately, the Kesslers have about died out. Only one daughter remains, and she lives in California somewhere. She didn't like living in McCray County, so she sold the original Kessler home places, the two stone houses on Kessler Boulevard where Josh and Richard have their offices."

"I saw them this afternoon. What about the sheriff's house? Is it a family home place too?"

"Not really. Daniel's grandfather on his mother's side was once the town's sole doctor, and he built that house so he would be near his patients. When Daniel got his degree in criminal justice and came back here to run for sheriff, his Grandfather Barbour had just retired and was preparing to move to Florida. He suggested Daniel live in the house. That way he would be close to his office and have plenty of room for his cats."

"And that suited Daniel?"

"Yes, he'd always loved that old place. Besides, there was no one else in the family to take on the responsibility. Daniel's the only offspring in his generation. The last McCray and the last Barbour. Bob and I had hoped to have children, but it wasn't meant to be."

Megan watched the older woman's eyes well up. "I'm sorry," she murmured, then quickly complimented her hostess on the cheese grits in hopes of distracting her. It didn't work.

"I'll give you the recipe, dear," Miss Evelyn murmured. "But back to Daniel. He doesn't have to make his home in Barbourville but I know he could never be happy anywhere else. He loves the town, the county, the people, the way of life. In fact, when Kaitlin . . ." She gave herself a visible shake. "Just listen to me, rambling on about family matters when I don't even have dessert on the table. Will you help me cut the pecan pies, my dear?"

"I'd be delighted," Megan said, and followed her hostess to the kitchen.

When Megan awoke the next morning, she could barely remember the end of the previous evening. She had been close to exhaustion by the time she climbed into the canopied bed in her spacious bedroom at Beth Ann's, and she had fallen asleep almost instantly. Now, with sunlight pouring through the window, she realized that this was the day she was scheduled to begin her four weeks of community service.

But how, when, and where?

She pushed herself out of bed and stumbled to the door, recalling that Beth Ann had indicated she should use the bathroom at the end of the hall. She opened the door and stifled a scream. Standing directly outside her door, his arm raised as though to knock, was a young man who could only be Beth Ann's son. Trevor had his mother's red hair, although his was a shade darker, and a band of freckles stretched from cheekbone to cheekbone. He regarded Megan solemnly out of green eyes that were slightly narrowed.

She blinked, trying to force herself awake. "Good morning," she murmured.

"You gonna make me read on my summer vacation?" Trevor's eyes narrowed a fraction more.

Megan forced her own eyes wider, suddenly aware that she was facing a challenge. Obviously Trevor was less enthused about the tutoring plan than his mother had been. "I'm planning to tutor you," she admitted, "but I hope to make it fun."

"I've already read *Moby Dick* and I don't want to read it again!"

"You've read *Moby Dick?* The whole thing?"

"Yes, and I didn't like it."

"I don't blame you. I read it when I was a senior in college, and I had a rough time getting through it. I would be amazed if you had liked it."

Trevor's eyes brightened. "Really?"

"Really. I'm eager to talk to you about our plans, Trevor, but first I need to dress and get a cup of coffee."

Trevor nodded. "Momma sent me up here to tell you there's coffee on the screened-in porch."

"She's an angel. Tell her I'll be down shortly."

After a quick shower, Megan dressed in a pair of slacks and a knit shirt from Beth Ann's shop, hoping the casual outfit would be appropriate for whatever the day was to bring. She didn't really know what to expect that day, but she wasn't prepared for the sight that greeted her when she stepped onto the screened-in porch.

Daniel was seated at a wicker table with a cup of coffee in his hand. His uniform was crisply pressed, his hair was neatly combed, and his face was freshly shaved. He smelled faintly of the lemony aftershave that Megan remembered from the previous day. The sheriff himself was especially appealing this morning, she decided. Not that he would welcome any interest from a rich city girl, she reminded herself.

But then he looked up, flashed Megan a charming smile, and stood. "Good morning, Miss

Marsh. As you can see, Beth Ann has set out a hearty breakfast. Whenever I have time before going to work, like this morning, I step across the street and mooch a cup of coffee off of her. Sometimes I even let her talk me into having a bite to eat." He grinned, then motioned toward a small buffet loaded with fresh fruit, bagels, and cream cheese. "Help yourself."

"I'll just have coffee to start with," Megan said, pouring a cup from the carafe. "I need to wake up before I eat."

"Are you one of those people who won't admit to being human before they've had their morning coffee?"

Megan smiled and shook her head. "I'm just a bit groggy this morning. I slept like the dead last night."

"I can understand that! My family exhausts me on a regular basis."

Megan laughed. "I didn't mean that, and you know it."

Daniel's smile faded. "Speaking of family, isn't there someone you would like to call to let them know you're safe? You're welcome to use the phone at the office to notify anyone you wish."

"Thanks anyway, but I used my cell phone last night to call a friend. She'll get in touch with my family. So, Sheriff, what are the plans for today?"

Daniel recognized a blatant change of subject

when it was flung across the breakfast table at him, and he decided to acquiesce gracefully. He intended to place some phone calls when he got back to the office anyway. He couldn't in good conscience allow Miss Marsh to mingle with his friends and family until he was positive she was as harmless as she appeared to be.

"Beth Ann and I have been talking about the plans for today. She has some time before opening the shop, so she's phoning some of the parents of the youngsters who need tutoring. If the parents are interested in meeting you, I'll drive you to their house or office and introduce you."

"Is chauffeuring a part of the sheriff's responsibilities?"

"Only when the sheriff's uncle has coerced an unsuspecting visitor into working for the county free of charge for the next month."

Megan laughed and helped herself to a bagel. "I just hope the other students aren't as nonplussed by this plan as Trevor appears to be."

Daniel looked up quickly. "What do you mean?"

"He isn't thrilled about being tutored during his summer vacation. And strangely enough, he seemed to think we might be undertaking literature such as *Moby Dick*. Surely I misunderstood him, but I could have sworn he said he had already read that epic. I can't imagine anyone assigning *Moby Dick* to eleven-year-olds."

"But then you haven't met their teacher, Mrs. Moulton. She appears to believe that literature can only consist of books that were written at least a hundred years ago. I recall plowing through Hawthorne when I was twelve. It was not a pleasant experience."

"I would imagine not. Mrs. Moulton obviously is from the old school of thought about what constitutes good literature. I prefer to assign students reading material that they're interested in."

"You sound as though you've had a great deal of experience."

"Not really. I've never held down a full-time teaching job even though I do have a degree in education and certification to teach in Georgia. However, I've done quite a bit of volunteer work with literacy programs."

"What kind of literature do you assign?"

"Sometimes the Bible. Sometimes *Sports Illustrated.* It depends on the student's age, reading level, and interests. I've even used a tomato soup can, but that was to address a situation the student considered an emergency."

Daniel nodded. "Interesting. I doubt Mrs. Moulton would approve, but these kids need help, and it sounds as though you're on the right track to help them."

Beth Ann appeared in the doorway. "Megan may be on the right track," she said, blinking rapidly, "but the train has already been derailed. Every parent I talked to refuses to participate because they've heard that Megan should be in jail instead of being allowed to corrupt the county's children. I tried to explain the situation to them, but they're not interested in the truth, only in the rumors that Horace Barnhart is spreading all over town."

Megan very carefully placed her bagel back on the plate in front of her. "I'm sorry you were put in the middle here, Beth Ann. I hope these people don't feel hard at you for calling them about me."

"Ha!" Beth Ann bounded into the room. "I'm not a redhead for nothing, you know. I told them exactly what I think about anyone who would believe gossip circulated by Horace Barnhart. One or two agreed to think it over, but I doubt we'll hear back from them." She heaved a deep sigh and plopped into a chair at the table.

Megan turned to Daniel. "What do I do now, Sheriff—pick up trash alongside the highway?"

"No, you'll continue with your plans to work with Trevor and not worry about the rest. The folks in this county know Horace Barnhart well enough not to be swayed by his opinions for very long."

Beth Ann sat up straight. "You're right, Daniel. When folks see that you and me and all the McCrays accept Megan, they'll figure Horace was just blowing everything out of proportion as usual."

"Exactly. So I'll go with Miss Marsh and Trevor this morning to round up some materials for their tutoring session. Then we'll all meet at the diner for lunch, and maybe Miss Marsh can help you out in the store this afternoon."

"But what about Trevor?" Megan asked. "I don't want him to work with me if that's going to make him an outcast with the other kids in town."

Trevor stepped through the open doorway and walked up beside his mother. "I was in the next room and heard what's going on. Don't worry about me, Miss Megan. I want to be a better reader, and it sounds like you'll be a good teacher. Do you think I could start off with *Sports Illustrated* like you mentioned a few minutes ago?"

Beth Ann patted her foot. "How long have you been eavesdropping, young man?"

"Just since you folks have been talking, Mom."

"Oh well, if that's all . . ." Beth Ann shrugged, then grinned and punched Trevor on the arm.

He returned his mother's grin but quickly turned back to Megan. "I think I'd like learning from a sports magazine if it's all the same to you."

"We'll walk over to the drugstore right after breakfast and you can pick out whatever interests you most."

"Yippee! Thanks, Miss Megan. I'm really going to like having you for a tutor. I'd better go put my shoes on." He dashed out of the room.

"Congratulations, Meg!" Beth Ann jumped up and gave Megan a quick hug. "You've already got my son interested in reading. Thank you! Now I've got to get ready to open the shop. Call me if you need me. Otherwise, I'll see you at the diner at lunchtime."

Daniel stood too. "I'll walk you and Trevor to the drugstore and help him pick out a couple of magazines. That is, if you don't mind the company."

Megan didn't mind the company. She knew she should mind the company. She knew she should avoid Sheriff Daniel McCray every time she possibly could.

But what she should do and what she wanted to do were at opposite ends of the spectrum, and she just didn't have the willpower this morning to do what she should.

"I'd love to have the company," she said, and was so thrilled to see Daniel's eyes light up that somehow the problems of the day suddenly seemed of no significance at all.

Chapter Six

"Daniel called to say he'll be here soon to pick you up." Beth Ann walked over to the breakfast buffet and poured an extra cup of coffee. "It's great that the Petrees and the Johnsons want to meet you already. You've only been tutoring Trevor for three days."

Megan pushed her breakfast plate to one side, smiled, and picked up the sheet of notebook paper she had reviewed during breakfast. "I'm pleased too. But just wait until you see how many vocabulary words Trevor has learned. And only half of them are related to sports."

"Trevor's bragged to everybody he sees about how much he likes being tutored. And since you

68

just work with him half a day, he's got time for the other stuff he likes to do."

Daniel's voice sounded from the doorway. "Anybody know where a sheriff can get a cup of coffee around here?"

Beth Ann winked at Megan. "I hear Sonny down at the diner makes a good cup of coffee," she shot back, then laughed. "Come on in, you moocher. I saw you coming across the street."

Daniel stepped into the breakfast parlor and accepted the cup Beth Ann already had poured for him. "Thanks! Did you give Miss Marsh the good news?"

"Sure did. You realize, don't you, Daniel, that if the Petrees and the Johnsons accept Megan, the Westons won't be far behind?"

"I suspect you're right, but first things first. We're supposed to be at the Petrees' house at nine o'clock and the Johnsons' place at ten. All of them are making it a point to stay at home until we arrive. Are you ready, Miss Marsh?"

Megan glanced down at her blue cotton skirt and coordinated knit shirt. "Am I dressed okay, Beth Ann?"

"Don't worry, Meg, you look just fine. Call me at the shop when you get back and let me know how things went."

Five minutes later Megan and Daniel were in

his car headed out of town. The morning air felt relatively cool, but the cloudless sky hinted at a warm day to come. "How far do we have to go?" Megan asked.

"The Petrees live on a small farm about fifteen miles out in the county," Daniel replied. "After we finish there, we'll swing back by the Johnsons' house. They live in a subdivision on the edge of town."

"It's kind of you to go with me."

"No problem."

"What did you find out when you checked up on me?"

Daniel's knuckles whitened where he grasped the steering wheel, but he showed no other sign of surprise. "What makes you think I checked up on you?"

"Well, even though you never asked me for the name of my alma mater, you're a sheriff, for heaven's sake. There must be dozens of ways you can get information about people. And, frankly, I don't think you'd be taking me into people's homes if you didn't already know quite a bit about me."

Daniel remained silent for a few seconds, then shrugged. "Your father is Allen Marsh. He and his two older brothers, Donald and Ray, have a successful law firm specializing in corporate law. You're an only child and have never been in trouble. On the contrary, you're known in Atlanta for your volunteer work with several charities."

Megan nodded. "Anything else?"

"You've never been married and never held down a full-time job. You still live at home and always have—except for your four years at Emory University. You belong to a prestigious country club. You have a generous allowance from your father and you shop at all the right stores."

"Is there anything you don't know?"

"I don't know why your father isn't camped out in my office threatening to sue McCray County on your behalf for false imprisonment."

"He doesn't know where I am. When I called my friend Jill and asked her to let him know I'm safe, I also told her not to give him my location."

"Why?"

Megan shrugged. "You know almost everything anyway so I might as well tell you the rest. Dad and I had a disagreement over the future direction of my life. He's a man who needs to feel in control of every situation. Twenty years ago when my mother contracted cancer, he discovered he couldn't control her disease and he couldn't save her. It shook him badly. Because I was all he had left, he was determined to protect me. He works at it a little too hard sometimes."

"I assume you agreed to Uncle Bob's plan so

you could prove something. Was it to yourself or to your father?"

"Both, I suppose, but mostly to me."

"That means you're using McCray County as much as McCray County is using you."

"More, probably. I don't know how much good I'll be to McCray County, but I've discovered a place that feels like a second home to me and met people who could easily become my friends for life."

Daniel nodded, then turned the steering wheel sharply to the right and pulled off the blacktop onto a rutted lane that wound through overhanging oaks, maples, and hemlocks. An understory of dogwoods, redbuds, and mountain laurel turned the landscape into a magical mixture of white and varying shades of green. The ruts continued for nearly half a mile before the road ended at the top of a cliff. A spreading valley of rolling hills lay below them.

Megan's eyes widened. "Where are we?"

"I thought this short side trip might be of interest to you." Daniel cut the motor. "Would you like to get out of the car a minute? The view from the top of the bluff is really impressive."

Megan suspected that the view wasn't the only thing on Daniel's mind. Nor, truth be told, was it foremost in her own thoughts. "I'd love to."

She waited for him to come around and open

her door, then gave him her hand and allowed him to help her out of the car. Neither made any effort to drop hands while they walked over uneven ground to the edge of the bluff.

The air was refreshingly cool. It was also heavy with the piney scent of evergreen trees and the musty odor of moist earth. A sudden breeze swept up and over the cliff, surprising Megan with a blast of dampness that chilled her.

Her breath caught in her throat as she looked out over the valley and the rolling hills that faded slowly into the hazy distance. Not even a spiral of smoke rose from the valley floor to hint at some trace of civilization, and a sudden flicker of fear, some primitive evocation of the vast unknown, sent a shiver down her spine. She dropped Daniel's hand and wrapped her arms around her bodice in an unconscious gesture of self-protection.

A quick frown touched his forehead. "Are you all right?"

"It's . . . I don't know how to describe it. Intimidating, I suppose. Do you feel anything like that when you look at this view?"

Daniel nodded. "Always. As you said, it's hard to describe, but I sometimes think that one of my ancestors must have stood in this very spot and looked out over that valley and wondered what on earth the future held for him."

Megan dropped her arms to her sides. "That's it

exactly," she said, relief in her voice. "It's as though I've had some past connection with the land, some tie that transcends time." She reached for his hand and was relieved when he quickly responded, grasping and warming her hand with his body heat.

"What's this area called?" Megan asked.

"Nothing original, I'm afraid. The bluff is called Buzzard's Roost, and the land below is known as Painter Valley. Some say it's named after an early settler. I like to think it's named for the mountain lions that once roamed this area. Oldtimers called them painters, which was the way they pronounced the word panther."

"I like your theory better. It's much more romantic."

"Speaking of romance . . ." Daniel reached for her other hand and pulled her gently toward him. She went willingly, leaning into him, lifting her face for the kiss she hoped was coming.

He didn't disappoint her. He lowered his head slowly. She didn't pull away, didn't want to pull away. This kiss was something she needed because she had thought so very many times about that first kiss, had wondered about it so often. Had she merely been tired that day? Or flustered? Or disoriented? Or had that kiss been every bit as wonderful as she recalled?

The instant his lips touched hers she knew the

answer. It was wonderful again, as wonderful as she had hoped it would be. Her blood heated in her veins and carried sparks throughout her body. She pulled her hands free of his and wrapped her arms around him, drawing herself against him.

She parted her lips and Daniel availed himself of the invitation. Megan tasted a hint of Beth Ann's coffee combined with Daniel's very own tantalizing flavor. She had burrowed even closer when suddenly a shadow passed over them. She half screamed, pulled back, and looked up.

The wingspread of the bird was not as broad as the shadow it cast, thank goodness. But it was an ugly thing, even considering the haunting grace of its soft and silent glide. Daniel wrapped an arm around Megan's shoulders and they watched in silent admiration while their visitor soared toward the valley and disappeared into the treetops.

"You see now why they call this Buzzard's Roost," Daniel said. He glanced at his watch. "We have to go. The Petrees are expecting us at nine o'clock and it's eight forty-five now."

"Yes." Megan sighed. "We have to go." She was shaken by her strong physical reaction to Daniel McCray. She wasn't sure what to make of her feelings, but when she gave him her hand so he could help her over the rough ground, her concerns vanished. Whatever this was, it felt right.

They walked in silence to the car. Daniel

opened her door, then grasped her shoulders and turned her to face him. "We can't pretend there's nothing between us, Megan," he said. "I don't know that either of us wants anything to come of it, but I think we owe it to ourselves to become better acquainted. Will you have dinner at my house tonight? I'm not a great cook, but I can grill a steak with the best of them. And you would have an opportunity to meet Eisenhower."

Megan lifted her brows. "Now there's an enticement I can't turn down. Not everyone can say they've met Eisenhower."

"Great," Daniel said, smiling. "That's great." His smile faded. "But in the meantime, we've got people to see. Let's go."

During the remainder of their drive, Megan listened carefully while Daniel filled her in on the families they were going to visit. Both the Petrees and the Johnsons had only one child, a son. The Petree boy, Mark, was Trevor's age, and Toby Johnson was a year younger. Both, Daniel said, appeared to be bright boys who had simply fallen behind in reading.

Although Megan's stomach had tightened with nerves when Daniel turned into the driveway of the Petrees' farmhouse, Amy and Charles Petree soon put her at ease. They were obviously loving parents who wanted the best for their son, and they expressed their appreciation for Megan's offer to tutor Mark.

"Sorry we didn't take you up on the offer immediately, Miss Marsh," Charles Petree said. "That Horace Barnhart got his facts mixed up, as usual, and it took us parents a day or two to get the straight of what you were offering to do for our kids. We appreciate you helping the kids out over the summer. Just a second, and I'll holler for Mark."

Mark Petree was a small but handsome boy with blond hair and large blue eyes. He was reluctant to talk at first, but Megan was accustomed to working with people who thought reading wasn't reading unless it involved the classics. When Mark discovered he could read anything that interested him, he quickly described his desire to become an architect, an ambition that startled both his parents. Since Megan knew next to nothing about architecture, she suggested they meet at the library the next morning to search for some books on the topic. Mark agreed with a broad grin on his face.

Megan's second potential student, little Toby Johnson, also described an interest that was foreign to Megan. Having never followed professional football, she was a bit dismayed to learn that Toby hoped someday to play in the NFL. While

Megan wasn't certain he would ever grow that much, she would never discourage any child's ambitions, so she suggested he join her and Mark the next morning to see what the library could offer on the topic. Toby, along with his parents, Claudia and Arnold, agreed to the idea with smiles and a promise to meet at the library at 10:00 the following morning.

Megan had Daniel drop her off at Beth Ann's store so she could report in person about the morning's successes.

"That's great, Meg." Beth Ann was practically jumping up and down. "But just you wait until you hear who called me while you were gone."

Megan's mouth turned dry. She feared that her father or one of his brothers had shown up in Barbourville, and she simply didn't feel up to dealing with any of her family yet. She wanted more time in McCray County to get to know the people, to get to know herself, and, especially, to get to know Daniel McCray. She moistened her lips. "Who?"

"Harold Davis," Beth Ann announced, a triumphant lilt in her voice.

Megan frowned in confusion. "Who?"

"Harold Davis is none other than the superintendent of McCray County Schools, and he is interested in talking to you about tutoring his daughter, Stacy." Beth Ann's grin widened. "That, my dear Meg, is a coup of the first order but I didn't want to sound too eager so I told him you were tied up today but would call him tomorrow."

Megan gave Beth Ann a quick hug. "You're a great friend, Beth Ann. I don't know how to thank you for everything."

Beth Ann's face turned a shade darker than her hair. "Pooh! I haven't done anything special. Look at all you're doing for Trevor."

"Trevor! I almost forgot our session. I'll bet he's at the house waiting for me! I'd better get on over there." She hurried to the door, then turned around. "By the way, Beth Ann."

"Yes?"

"I won't be home for supper tonight. Daniel has invited me to have steaks with him."

Beth Ann's eyebrows shot up. "Just the two of you?"

Megan silently cursed the blush she felt warming her face. "Yes, I think so."

"Okay," Beth Ann said, nodding her head rapidly. "Sure. No problem!" She turned quickly and began sliding hangers around on a rack, but not before Megan had spotted her friend's delighted smile. She groaned softly and slipped out of the shop.

The tutoring session with Trevor went well. He was proving to be a bright and willing student since Megan had tapped into a topic that interested him. She felt very optimistic about Trevor being able to move ahead at least two grade levels in reading before the summer ended.

They worked until noon when Megan excused Trevor to join his friends. Megan decided to skip lunch at the diner, mostly because she was afraid Beth Ann would drop hints about the upcoming evening to everyone who set foot in the restaurant. Instead, she fixed herself a sandwich, then hunted up some work gloves in the garage and went outside to weed the flagstone path. The sun was warm, but Megan made sure she worked in the shade, and a soft breeze kept her cool. When the path was finished, she scrounged around until she found a pair of hedge trimmers. By late afternoon she felt hot and sweaty, but Beth Ann's yard showed definite signs of improvement.

Megan had just stepped out of the shower a half-hour later when Beth Ann called to her through the bathroom door. "Daniel called. He said to join him in his backyard around seven. I can see smoke rising over there, so he must have the barbecue lit."

"Okay." Megan wrapped herself in a towel and opened the door. "What did you think of the yard?"

"That I'd come home to the wrong address. What are you trying to do, kill yourself?"

"Actually, I was trying to work off an unusually severe case of nerves."

"About this evening?"

Megan sighed. "Am I rushing things, Beth Ann? I've not even known Daniel for a week."

"Meg, you're just having dinner with him. Don't turn it into a federal case."

"You're right. Of course, you're right. It's just dinner." She smiled. "Thanks, Beth Ann. I'd better dry my hair now."

She closed the bathroom door and leaned back against it. Tonight was more than a dinner. She knew that. She also knew she was juggling several sticks of dynamite and that events tonight just might light the fuses.

Fuses being lit. Whoops! That imagery was a little too close for comfort. She and Daniel seemed to light each other's fuses much too easily, and a mutual conflagration wouldn't be good for either one of them.

She would be in McCray County for only three and a half more weeks. And Daniel was only interested in local women. Besides that, he didn't even like her type. He had told her as much right after he kissed her that first time and made her forget what part of the world she was in.

So why was she going? Megan shook her head and reached for the hair dryer. Darn if she knew.

She flipped the switch and began blowing hot air on the style Andre had created for her just last week. No, she didn't know why she was going. She only knew that if she was playing with explosives, she was willing to risk the big bang.

Fifteen minutes later, after Beth Ann had approved of her tan shorts, plaid blouse, and beige sandals, Megan walked across Redbud to Daniel's large Victorian. Unlike Beth Ann's place, Daniel's showed no signs of neglect. The house was painted a green so soft it came close to being white, and the Victorian details—the fish-scale shingles, the gingerbread gable brackets, the turned balusters on the second-floor balcony—all looked in perfect condition.

The grounds were neat too. A soft green lawn surrounded the meandering brick pathway that led both to the front door and also around the side of the house toward a gate in the picket fence. When the fence ended, a thick yew hedge took over. Potted begonias and impatiens lined the pathway, and climbing roses and clematis scrambled up and over an arbor at the far side of the front entrance.

"Come on back!" Daniel yelled. He opened the gate and motioned Megan through. "How do you like my apron?" He wore it over a pair of jeans and a soft blue T-shirt.

Megan concluded there ought to be a law against a man looking that good, especially when he was wearing an apron. She paused and cocked her head to one side to examine the item of apparel Daniel seemed so proud of. It was a white bib-type, printed in dark blue. Megan read the message and groaned. "I ought to turn around and go home right now."

Daniel grinned, a bit impishly. "You don't like it?"

"Like it? A drawing of a guy standing beside a cold barbecue grill and saying, 'Come light my fire?' Good thing you're the sheriff. Such atrocious taste must be against the law."

Daniel laughed. "Sorry. I couldn't resist. Uncle Bob gave it to me for Christmas last year."

"Now why doesn't that surprise me?"

"Maybe because you've met Uncle Bob. Anyway, the fire is already lit and the steaks are cooking. The salad's in the refrigerator, and I've got corn on the cob and baking potatoes on the grill. We'll eat on the screened-in porch to avoid the bugs."

"Sounds wonderful. Can I do anything?"

"Just relax." Daniel nodded toward a white rope hammock between two trees. "Make yourself comfortable. Or, if you prefer, I'll give you the deluxe, three-minute tour of the yard."

"I'll take a rain check on the tour. After working in Beth Ann's yard all afternoon, I'm a bit saturated with plants. That hammock looks good to me."

"Do you know how to get into one?"

"Good grief, how hard can it be?" Megan marched over to the hammock, turned around, backed up to the edge, and plopped down. A second later, she was lying on her face in the grass.

"Are you all right?" Daniel had dashed over and dropped to one knee beside her. Megan glanced up just in time to see him wipe a huge told-you-so grin off his face.

"An evil witch must have cast a spell on every seating contraption in McCray County," Megan said, a bitter edge to her tone. She flipped over onto her back. "I never realized before that sitting down can be so dangerous."

Daniel laughed out loud. "You do have a poor track record in that regard. Maybe I'd better help you into the hammock. It can be a little tricky."

"No kidding?"

"Sorry." Daniel was still grinning. "On the other hand, it can be really comfortable once you get settled in."

Megan's sigh was long-suffering. "Okay. Show me the proper procedure."

"Give me your hands." Daniel pulled Megan to her feet. "Okay, you turn around and back up to the hammock like this."

Megan plopped her hands onto her hips. "I did that—just like that. Exactly like that."

"I know, but it's the next part that's tricky.

Come over here beside me and I'll illustrate. It's one of those things you need to get a feel for."

Megan sighed but did as Daniel asked. She soon stood beside him with her backside resting on the edge of the hammock.

"Now place your hands on the hammock about this far back from the edge. That's good! Now pull the hammock under you as you sit down. Now!"

A second later they were both face down in the grass. Megan giggled, then laughed out loud. "The mighty hammock tamer bites the dust—I mean the grass," she declared before quickly rolling out of Daniel's reach.

He pretended to snarl, then started getting to his feet. "I won't be defeated by this thing, and I won't allow you to be defeated by it either. Come on."

"Count me out, Captain Ahab." Holding her hands in front of her, palms out in a defensive gesture, Megan backed away a few steps. "You and that Great White Hammock may be locked in a battle to the death, but I have my own furniture demons to deal with. Once you've been in the clutches of a bottom-eating chair, you're doubly cautious around furniture that shows signs of being carnivorous."

Daniel patted the swaying hammock. "See? Gentle as a lamb, I promise you. Come back over here."

Megan approached slowly. "No more dumping?"

"You have its word."

"Could I have your word as well?"

"That I won't dump you? Absolutely."

"Okay." Megan stopped pretending to be frightened and backed up to the hammock again. This time, after surviving a few bucks and wild swings, she and Daniel ended up in the center of the hammock in a tangle of arms and legs, too weak from laughter to do more than rest against each other until their chuckles faded away.

Somehow Megan's hand had landed on Daniel's left bicep. She couldn't resist. She squeezed gently. She could hear his breath catch and a smile slipped onto her face. She liked knowing she could affect him so easily, liked knowing she wasn't alone in her physical reactions to their closeness.

"Putting the squeeze on the law?" Daniel whispered. His mouth had ended up right next to Megan's ear, and she shivered when she felt him nibble gently on her lobe.

Megan squeezed a little harder. "That's what it feels like to me."

"I may have to take you in for this, you know." Daniel's mouth eased downward and he began dropping tiny kisses on the side of Megan's neck.

"Mmmm, I hope so." She eased her head around until they were face to face and Daniel's lips were opposite hers. He moved toward her slowly, giving her ample time to pull away, but Megan didn't want to pull away. However foolhardy it might be, she couldn't resist kissing him again. Surely this time, it would be just another kiss. Surely this time there would be no fireworks, no explosions.

This time was more potent than ever. Sparklers appeared behind Megan's closed eyes and sent stickles of fire racing through her bloodstream. She couldn't help wondering if Daniel was feeling anything nearly as strong as she was.

Daniel couldn't believe it was happening again, only this time with even more power than the first two times he had kissed Megan Amelia Marsh. What in the world was he thinking? They had no future. She was a city girl who would be going back to her socialite life in a little over three weeks. He was a country boy, pure and simple, and he wanted nothing more than to live out his life in McCray County.

Yet kissing Megan made him forget that anything had value beyond being with her, listening to her laugh, watching the changing expressions in her eyes. Holding her in his arms.

It wasn't easy, but he managed to pull her closer without tipping them into the grass. She responded by cuddling against him.

He deepened their kiss, and Megan moaned

softly. He threw his right leg across her. She pushed an elbow into the hammock, levering herself half on top of him. He pulled his right arm out from under her so he could wrap it around her and pull her even closer.

A voice sounded from the back corner of the house. "Looks to me like something's getting a little too hot back here."

Daniel sprang away from Megan so quickly that the hammock bucked, tossing both of them into the grass.

"Blast it all, Uncle Bob!" Daniel shouted. He pushed himself up onto his elbows and glared at the county judge. "You scared me half to death."

The judge widened his eyes in a maneuver obviously intended to portray wounded surprise. "I called out when I was in the front yard, but you didn't answer. Then, when I stepped on back here, I couldn't help noticing that your grill's smoking pretty bad. I merely commented on the imminent end of your T-bones."

"Bloody hell," Daniel said through clenched teeth. He scrambled to his feet and held out a hand to help Megan stand. Only then did he notice she still lay on her stomach and that her entire body was shaking. "Megan? Are you crying?"

She flipped over onto her back. Laughter had brightened her eyes and brought a soft glow to her cheeks. Daniel wanted nothing more than to drop onto the grass beside her and take up where they had left off, but his Uncle Bob still stood beside the smoking grill, watching them with a sly smile in his eyes.

"Don't mind me." Megan wiped tears of laughter from her eyes. "Rescue the steaks and find out what your uncle wants."

"I know what he wants," Daniel said under his breath. He hurried over to the grill and grabbed the barbecue fork. "He wants what he always wants, to make my life a living hell."

"Did you mutter something, Danny boy?" The judge's smile was a study in innocence.

Daniel forked a black steak and waved it under his uncle's nose. "Why yes, I was inviting you to join us for supper."

The judge made a point of looking for a few seconds at Megan, who still lay under the hammock. "No thanks. I just dropped by to ask if you were monitoring Miss Marsh's activities. I think I can see for myself that you are." He smiled broadly and waved at Megan. "Bye now, Miz Marsh."

Megan sat up and waved back. "Good-bye Judge McCray."

Daniel suppressed a desire to fling the burned steak at his uncle's back. Instead he dropped it into the trashcan and walked over to help Megan stand. "Did I hear you say you were in the mood for pizza tonight?"

"Absolutely." Megan grinned. "You get the phone and I'll look up the number."

Chapter Seven

"I'm glad to see you looking rested," Beth Ann said when Megan stepped into the breakfast parlor the next morning. "Of course you should, considering how early you got in last night." She set a plate heaped with sliced cantaloupe on the table and turned to regard Megan with raised eyebrows.

Megan grinned. "To answer your unspoken question, no, Daniel and I didn't argue last night. Unfortunately, my strenuous labors in your yard yesterday afternoon caught up with me and I was yawning even before the pizza arrived."

"Pizza? What pizza? I thought Daniel was grilling steaks."

"Long story. Wow, Beth Ann, this breakfast buffet looks wonderful. I hope you're not going to all this trouble every morning on my account."

"Not a very subtle change of subject, my dear Meg!" Beth Ann curled her nose in mock disapproval. "But don't worry. I fix a nice breakfast to start Trevor off with a healthy meal."

"Good. I wouldn't want you going to extra trouble for me."

"Now that we've covered that topic, let's get back to last night. What happened to the steaks?"

"They burned."

"Ah! I'll bet this *is* a long story! Care to start at the beginning?"

"No, because I don't have time. I've got to call the school superintendent before meeting the Petrees and Johnsons at the library to pick out reading materials for Mark and Toby."

"Okay, but you're not off the hook for good, my slithery friend."

"Understood." Megan grabbed a bagel and hurried over to the wall phone near the door. The superintendent answered on the first ring and Megan invited him and his daughter to visit the tutoring session that would begin in Beth Ann's parlor around 11:00. He assured her they would be there.

Megan and Beth Ann left the house at the same time, Beth Ann to open her shop and Megan to walk to the town library. Trevor was staying at home to prepare for the upcoming tutoring session.

The Petrees and Johnsons were waiting for Megan and the boys were already scouring the shelves for books they wanted to read. Megan helped each in turn, and by the time both had selected appropriate reading materials, it was almost eleven. Megan quickly explained to the Petrees and Johnsons why she was in a bit of a hurry, and both sets of parents expressed delight that Stacy Davis was going to be joining the tutoring sessions. Claudia Johnson explained that Stacy's mother had died three years earlier when Stacy was ten, and that Stacy had started falling behind in school at that time.

Megan turned down offers of a ride from both the Petrees and the Johnsons, preferring to walk back to Beth Ann's so she would have a few minutes to get acquainted with the boys before starting the tutoring session. Mark was quieter than Toby, so Megan made a point of asking him about his interests beyond architecture. She couldn't suppress a shiver when he announced that he loved collecting bugs. "Interesting," she murmured and quickly turned to ask Toby what he liked besides football.

When the trio turned onto Redbud Road, Mark skipped ahead a few paces, then stopped and pointed to a car sitting at the curb in front of Beth Ann's house. "Look. There's Stacy and her dad."

Megan took a deep breath. Meeting the school superintendent shouldn't unnerve her. After all, he had been perfectly amiable on the phone that morning. But she realized that his disapproval could sabotage all her tutoring efforts in McCray County.

Fortunately for her nerves, Harold Davis saw the group approaching and got out of his car, sporting a cheerful smile. "Morning, all," he called and went around to open his daughter's car door.

When Stacy Davis stepped onto the sidewalk, Megan saw that the girl was at an age when she was an awkward combination of too-big feet, too-long legs, and a skinny torso, all of which promised to someday become the type of body that graced magazine covers and fashion runways. Stacy's face was slender, and she had large brown eyes and a wide mouth with full lips that, at the moment, were pulled into a tight pout of anger.

Harold Davis strode up to Megan and held out his hand. "Miss Marsh! I'm so appreciative of the work you're doing here this summer. Beth Ann says it's amazing how much Trevor has progressed in less than a week."

"I can't take credit for that. Trevor has worked very hard, even though he doesn't see it as work because he's enjoying himself so much."

"Well, don't expect me to be as easily fooled as these babies," Stacy said. She glared at Megan while sticking out a lower lip and waving a skinny arm toward Mark and Toby.

"Hey!" Mark protested. "We're not babies, are we, Miss Megan?"

The superintendent spoke before Megan could answer. "No, Mark, you're not. And Stacy is going to apologize for that remark, aren't you, young lady?"

"I'm sorry," Stacy muttered, dropping her gaze and glaring at the sidewalk.

"Let's get out of this hot sun," Megan suggested, more anxious to cool tempers than bodies. "Mr. Davis, why don't you come back at noon to pick Stacy up. That should give her time to decide if she wants to join our group."

Stacy looked up quickly. "I have a choice?"

"We have choices about most things," Megan said. "And you certainly have a choice about working with me. I don't think I could teach someone who doesn't want to learn. So stick around a little while and if you don't want to come back tomorrow, that's fine with me."

Stacy's father opened his mouth as though to protest but quickly closed it when Megan caught his eye. He nodded. "I'll be back at noon," he said and left without another word.

By noon, all four of Megan's students were happily wrangling about who had chosen the most interesting topic. Trevor and Toby insisted that sports were the most fascinating. Mark agreed that some sports were fun, and Stacy admitted to enjoying women's basketball but not much else. What Stacy was most interested in, she finally told Megan, was archaeology, the field her mother had studied in college.

While Megan couldn't help wishing at least one of the students had chosen a subject she was even half familiar with, she was delighted that Stacy had finally expressed interest in something. Stacy even volunteered to go to the library that afternoon and look for some books or articles to bring with her the next morning. Megan agreed, pretending along with Stacy that there was never any doubt that she would return.

By the time Megan had wrapped up the morning session and waved the youngsters off for their afternoon activities, she was famished but decided to straighten up the parlor before fixing herself a sandwich. She was just stacking the reading materials on the shelf above the TV when she heard Daniel calling from the back door.

"Anybody home?"

"I'm in the parlor," Megan called back. "Come on in."

Daniel paused in the doorway. "How did your morning go?"

"Great." She told him about Stacy's initial reluctance. "I certainly wasn't going to push her, but with the three boys acting silly as only three boys can, she was soon laughing right along with the rest of us, and then she seemed to relax and begin enjoying herself. I think she must have been a very lonely little girl since her mother died."

"Does she know you lost your mother too?"

"It hasn't come up. I didn't want to make a point of it for fear she might think I was trying to create some artificial connection between us."

"You may be right. Anyway, it sounds as though you two are connecting on some level, which is good. But I'm about to forget my mission. Beth Ann said I was to bring you to the diner for lunch today. She's afraid if you stay here you'll wear yourself out in the lawn again."

"No such danger. I have no desire to . . ." She looked around quickly. "What's that racket?"

"Sounds like somebody's pounding on the front door, which is unusual. Most people either walk right in or ring the bell. You stay here. I'll check it out."

Megan ignored his instructions to stay put and fell in behind him while he hurried toward the front of the house. A renewed pounding suggested that whoever was at the front door was using a fist to beat on the solid wood.

"Don't knock the door down!" Daniel yelled. "I'll be there in a second!"

He turned the knob and jerked the door open. "Horace! What in blazes are you doing?"

Horace brushed past Daniel and stepped into the hallway. Perspiration ran in rivulets down his ruddy face, and his breath came in short puffs. "Miss Marsh. Thank goodness you're here. I came as fast as I could. You've got to hide. They've come for you."

Daniel slapped a hand onto his deputy's shoulder. "Calm down, man. What are you talking about? Who's come for Miss Marsh?"

Horace drew a deep breath, then stared at Megan with widened eyes. "I don't hold with drug running, Miss Marsh. But that must be what you've been doing or them men wouldn't be after you. They're in the sheriff's office now. I put them off, told them I'd have to see if you was still in town, but they mean business, I could tell that."

Daniel regarded his deputy with a puzzled frown. "Slow down, Horace. I can't make any sense out of what you're saying. Who's in my office?"

"Three gangsters looking for Miss Marsh. I'm scared they've come to get her because she didn't finish up her drug errands for them."

"How do you know they're gangsters?"

"Their mean looks, and the way they dress. All three are wearing them fancy suits with little stripes in the material, and they've all got on dark shirts and dark ties that match the shirts, and they said they was from Chicago. One said—his eyes was cold as death—he said if I didn't take him to Miss Marsh immediately, he'd start tearing this town apart brick by brick. And I believe he would."

Megan blew her breath out in a long sigh. "That sounds like Dayton."

"No ma'am." Horace shook his head. "Not Dayton. He said they was from Chicago for sure."

"I meant my *Uncle* Dayton," Megan explained. "I should have known that those three would browbeat poor Jill into telling them where I am. If they've upset her, I'll—"

"Excuse me, Megan. What three are we talking about here?"

"My uncles from Chicago." Megan shook her head and sighed in disgust. "I'm sure it's the triplets, my mother's younger brothers. They were only twelve when she died, and she asked them to watch over me. She couldn't have known they would take her words so literally. They've never allowed me to see a minute's peace."

"That characteristic seems to apply to all uncles," Daniel muttered, his tone verging on bitterness.

Megan nodded. "And I have so many of them. You have no idea what—"

"Excuse me, Miss Marsh," Horace interrupted, his eyes wide. "Are you saying that you're in the same family with those gangsters?"

"Get a grip, Horace," Daniel said. "It's not a crime family, and those men are not gangsters." He quickly turned to Megan. "Are they?"

"No, but Uncle Dallas would love knowing that Horace thought they were."

"Dallas?"

Megan grinned. "Yes."

"And Dayton?"

"Yes."

"Let me see if I can guess the third one's name. Hmmm. Detroit?"

"No, that would be silly. It's Denver."

"Of course. I should have known."

"Excuse me again!" Horace ran a finger around his collar. "I'm glad to see you two enjoying yourselves so much, but them three are back at the station, and they may not be gangsters but they sure did seem impatient to see Miss Marsh. What are we going to do?"

"Oh, I'd better go calm them down," Megan said. She glanced in the mirror in the hall and ran her fingers through her hair. "Honestly, I wish those three would marry and have children of their own to harass. Maybe then they would leave me alone."

"I don't think it works that way," Daniel said. "But it doesn't hurt to hope. Come on, I've got my car outside. I'll drive you to the office."

"I'm coming too," Horace announced, his chin jutting out. "Just in case they aren't who Miss Marsh thinks they are."

"Who else would . . . ?" Daniel began, then shrugged. "Oh never mind. Come on."

All three men waited on the concrete stoop outside the sheriff's office and stepped in unison toward the parking lot when Daniel pulled in. He instantly understood why Horace had been so upset. These three looked as though they could indeed be hit men. Tall, dark complected, with dark brown hair, square chins, and cold blue eyes, the brothers at first appeared identical. Another instant of observation revealed they were not.

The brother on the right was perhaps an inch taller than the other two and was, Daniel suspected, the leader of the trio. He held his shoulders just a bit straighter and his chin a little higher than the other two.

The middle brother also stood with his shoulders square. He was a bit more muscular than the others, and a half-smile tugged at the corners of his lips, giving the appearance that he was forever amused but struggled to appear solemn.

The third brother was set apart from the others by his slightly slouched posture and the suggestion in his eyes that he was bored beyond belief. His eyes were definitely a deeper blue than those of his brothers, and they were certainly colder. He stifled a yawn but quickly stood straighter when Daniel rolled to a stop and Megan got out of the car.

She was instantly surrounded by her uncles, and after tossing them one disgusted look, she began laughing and hugging them and declaring that she was going to go to court to file for a legal separation from them.

The legal separation comment was apparently a family joke, because the three brothers merely laughed and chided her for causing them worry.

"I hope to high heavens you didn't upset Jill," Megan said in a severe tone. She turned to glare at the tallest brother. "Uncle Dayton, you especially have always unnerved the poor girl. Did you frighten her to death in order to make her tell you where I was?"

The man Daniel thought of as the leader quickly raised his right hand. "You have my word that I was extremely polite to Jill. If I happened to mention that I had recently acquired some medieval torture devices and she happened to assume facts not in evidence, I can hardly be held to blame."

"I beg to differ, Uncle Dayton. I shall certainly hold you to blame."

"Let up on the poor boy, Meggie," the amused brother drawled. "Jill came out of their little encounter totally unscathed, as always. But aren't you going to introduce us to your new friends. Or would *captors* be a more appropriate term?"

"I beg your pardon, Uncle Denver. I'm forgetting my manners." She motioned Daniel and Horace forward. "And the correct terminology is definitely *friends*. They've been most kind. May I introduce the sheriff of McCray County, Daniel McCray, and his deputy, Horace Barnhart. Sheriff McCray, Deputy Barnhart, my uncles, Dayton, Denver, and Dallas."

The men shook hands all around. When that ritual was complete, Daniel invited the three brothers to step inside his office. Then he remembered the deplorable condition of his chairs and quickly suggested that they go to the diner instead.

Megan apparently understood the reason behind Daniel's quick change of plans. She caught his eye, nodded, and said, "Yes, please, let's go to the diner. I'm half-famished, and I suspect everyone could use a bite to eat."

Dayton gave a half-smile. "By all means, let's go to the diner, my dearest Megan. I would hate to be guilty of contributing to your demise through starvation."

"What did he say?" Horace whispered to Daniel.

"He wants some lunch," Daniel whispered back.

"A long-winded feller, ain't he?"

Dayton regarded Horace with raised eyebrows, then turned to Daniel. "Since I don't know the location of the diner, I'll drive my car and follow you, if that's agreeable with you, Sheriff."

"It's fine with me," Daniel said. "Let's go."

They had taken only two steps toward the parked cars when the loud and long screeching of tires brought the party to a quick halt.

"What in blue blazes?" Daniel murmured, watching Beth Ann wheel into the parking lot, slam on her brakes, and jump from the car. Her face was flushed, and her hair stood out from her head like a red tumbleweed. Obviously she had been driving with her window rolled down.

She ran toward the silently staring group and grabbed Daniel by the pocket of his uniform shirt. "Daniel McCray, don't you dare let them take Meg. You know she's innocent!"

"Relax, Beth Ann. Nobody's taking Megan any-where except to the diner for lunch." Daniel started carefully prying Beth Ann's fingers away from his pocket, hoping she wouldn't rip it off his shirt before he could calm her down.

"Lunch? But what about these gangsters? What are they doing here?"

"Gangsters?" A smile wiped the boredom from Dallas' face. "Is that what we are? Hot damn. I've always wanted to be a gangster."

Since he had just finished loosening Beth Ann's grip on his pocket, Daniel was able to grasp her hand in his and hold onto it. He had grown up with Beth Ann's temper, and he knew just how unpredictable she could be when she felt one of her friends was being threatened. He didn't want her to throw a left hook that could get her in trouble.

Fortunately, today she seemed to prefer regality to hostility. She straightened her shoulders and regarded Dallas with her head tipped to one side as though examining a strange specimen of the insect world. "Congratulations, sir. Your wish to become a gangster should be easily achieved. You dress the part at least."

"Thank you, madam. Unfortunately, I fear that you, like our little Meggie here, must be a prisoner of the county. Obviously you've both been issued the same atrocious prison garb. Frankly, I think a case could be made for cruel and unusual treatment."

Megan's gasp of dismay was immediately followed by Beth Ann's snort of outrage.

Dayton stepped forward. "I don't believe we've
been introduced, ma'am," he said, then flashed
Beth Ann a charming smile. "I'm Megan's uncle,
Dayton. The scoundrels who resemble me so
closely are, unfortunately, my brothers. The rude
one is Dallas. The other is Denver." He offered
Beth Ann his arm. "Allow me to escort you to the
diner, ma'am, and I'll explain our sudden arrival
in your charming town."

Beth Ann regarded Dayton solemnly, as though
finding him just as strange as his brother, but she
soon returned his smile and then, after a final glare
for Dallas, rested her hand on Dayton's proffered
arm and nodded regally.

Daniel stepped to Megan's side. "That was
close," he murmured. "I've seen Beth Ann rip the
hide off armadillos for less provocation."

"I wouldn't have blamed her," Megan responded softly. "Uncle Dallas was unbelievably rude.
I've never seen him behave that badly before."

"Maybe it's one of those instant personality
conflicts."

"I suppose," Megan said, a note of doubt in her
tone.

"I wouldn't worry. Your Uncle Dallas is probably just concerned about you. After all, all three of

them traveled from Chicago to check on you, and they still don't know what's going on."

"I'd better explain the situation to them," Megan said. "I don't want them thinking I was coerced into community service."

Daniel opened his car door for Megan. "Then perhaps you should *refrain* from explaining. They're bound to realize immediately that coercion is exactly what Uncle Bob had in mind."

"Say, can I bum a ride?"

Megan quickly turned toward her Uncle Denver who had stepped up behind her.

He gave her a quick smile. "It's getting a little crowded in the other car, not to mention a little tense. Beth Ann offered to drive and Dayton took her up on it, but her car's small and Deputy Barnhart takes up quite a bit of space. Not to mention the fact that Dallas insisted on riding in the front, and Beth Ann is being so polite to him, I'm afraid she'll explode before they reach the diner."

"No problem," Daniel said. "Climb in."

"Thanks." Denver got into the back seat and waited until Daniel had started the car and pulled out onto Kessler Boulevard before speaking. "Okay, Meggie, my dear," he said in a too-pleasant tone. "Why do I get the impression that you've been coerced into doing community ser-

vice here in McCray County? And why did I spot
your BMW locked up in an impoundment lot
behind Stubblefields' garage as we were coming
into town?"

Chapter Eight

"So long to The Three Ds, hello peace," Megan murmured. She stood beside Daniel in the parking lot of the sheriff's office and waved goodbye to her uncles as they pulled out onto Kessler Boulevard. They were headed back to Chicago because she had managed to convince them she was spending a month in McCray County of her own accord and, although they didn't seem thrilled, they accepted her decision. Her hand dropped to her side when Dayton turned a corner and the car moved out of sight. "I think that went fairly well, don't you?" she asked, turning toward Daniel.

Daniel's brows shot up. "Maybe, if you're willing to discount the fact that Dallas spent the after-

109

noon tossing barbs at Beth Ann, Denver watched me like I was Al Capone disguised as a county sheriff, and Dayton observed everybody and everything with a decidedly haughty attitude."

"What?" Megan gaped at him. "I don't know where you came up with those ideas. My uncles were perfectly polite to everyone the entire afternoon after that first little episode between Dallas and Beth Ann."

Daniel shrugged. "I guess you city folks define polite behavior a little differently than we do out here in the country."

"For heaven's sake!" A flash of anger heated Megan's face. Where had Daniel's sudden antagonism come from? "Don't you dare start pulling a good-old-country-boy act on me, Daniel McCray," she said, glaring at him. "I happen to know through your Aunt Evelyn that you are not only well educated but also more widely traveled than most city folks will ever be."

Daniel's eyes narrowed. "I'm not pulling any kind of act on you, Miss Marsh, but it doesn't take a genius to see that your uncles don't like the idea of you spending a month here. And if you approve of the way Dallas looked down his nose at Beth Ann all afternoon, you're not half the friend to her I thought you were. She may not be able to afford designer clothes, but that doesn't mean she's not a great person."

Megan pulled a deep breath into her lungs while her anger slowly gave way to distress. Nevertheless, she immediately lifted her chin. She would rather be staked out on an ice floe to freeze to death as to let Daniel see how deeply he had hurt her.

"As you said, Sheriff McCray, you are definitely not a genius. Anyone with half a mind could see that Dallas and Beth Ann were so deeply attracted to each other that they didn't know how to handle their feelings. And in case it escaped your attention, Beth Ann gave as good as she got."

Daniel's lips narrowed. "Attracted? If that's your idea of attraction, I hope I'm never attracted to anyone."

"So do I, Sheriff McCray," Megan said, thankful that her distress had now turned back into anger. "So do I. Now, if you'll excuse me, I'm going to walk back to Beth Ann's. I need the exercise, I'm afraid." She turned and, with squared shoulders, hurried across the parking lot and onto the sidewalk leading down Kessler Boulevard.

Unfortunately, by the time Megan reached the flagstone path leading to Beth Ann's porch, she had begun to wonder if Daniel had been right. Had Dallas spent the afternoon picking at Beth Ann? Had he hurt Beth Ann's feelings? Would Beth Ann be waiting to toss Megan out of her house?

Megan half expected to see her suitcases sitting

on the front porch. What would she do if Beth Ann was angry with her? She adored Beth Ann. She would never forgive Uncle Dallas if he had hurt her friend.

Dear heavens, Beth Ann had just stepped onto the front porch carrying something. Was it Megan's suitcase?

Megan breathed a sigh of relief. No, it was only an old-fashioned metal watering can. Beth Ann had come out to tend to the hanging baskets that lined the porch and she seemingly didn't see Megan approaching.

Or else she was pointedly ignoring her.

"Hello," Megan called out.

Beth Ann glanced at Megan, then reached to pull a brown leaf off the spider plant. "Hi."

Oh dear. Beth Ann was obviously angry. She had always greeted Megan effusively, not with a single word like "Hi."

Megan stopped at the edge of the porch. "How are the plants?"

Beth Ann tossed the leaf off the side of the porch and stared at Megan. "Thirsty, as usual for this time of year. How are you?"

"Worried."

Beth Ann set her watering can down with a thud. "Worried about what?"

"You. Are you upset because of the way Dallas treated you this afternoon?"

"Upset?" Beth Ann gaped at her. "Upset?" She grinned, then laughed out loud. "Are you kidding? I haven't had that much fun sparring with a man since Trevor's daddy passed on. Your uncle is one attractive man. And I could tell he liked me too. In fact, I haven't seen that many sparks flying since Granny hired Clarence Pennycuff to weld a crack in her iron wash kettle." Her grin quickly faded. "My God, Meg honey, what's wrong with you?"

Megan could not stop the tears running down her cheeks. She had obviously been much more tense than she realized. Now that she knew for sure that her uncle hadn't insulted her dear friend, the relief was more than she could deal with.

Beth Ann draped an arm around Megan's shoulder. "Come sit down in the glider, sweetheart, and I'll bring you a glass of iced tea. Then you can tell me what's wrong." She suddenly jumped back with a gasp. "Good heavens! Your uncles aren't making you go back home, are they?"

Megan shook her head. "No, no, it's nothing like that. It's just that, well, Daniel was convinced that Uncle Dallas had treated you horribly, and I was afraid that you were hurt and maybe mad at me too."

Beth Ann's eyes widened. "Mad at you? For heaven's sake, Meg, you should know better than that. And what, pray tell, gives Daniel McCray the right to comment on my flirtation with your uncle? I mean, if anyone had a right to object, it would be you."

Megan swiped away her tears. "Why would I object? I haven't seen Uncle Dallas that engrossed in a conversation in years. Most women just kind of shrivel up and fade away when he cuts loose with that tongue of his."

"Well I enjoyed it," Beth Ann said. "But what on earth possessed Daniel to complain?"

Megan sighed. "Long story."

"Good. Sit down in the glider and I'll get us both a glass of tea. Then you can fill me in on every detail. Be right back."

Fifteen minutes later, Beth Ann plopped her glass of tea onto the rattan table and paced the length of the porch. "I just can't believe Daniel was so hateful to you. He must be feeling insecure."

"Why on earth would he feel insecure?"

"Well, let's face it, Meg. Your uncles are not exactly country bumpkins. We've not had that level of sophistication in McCray County since, since, since . . ."

Beth Ann's sentence trailed off. She stared toward the street, where a bright red Jaguar had slowed to a crawl in front of her house. The driver's side window slid down, and a female with glittering blond hair leaned out and waved gaily. "Hi Beth Ann. I'm back." The woman glanced in her rearview mirror. "Traffic coming up behind me," she called. "See you soon." She speeded up and turned the corner from Redbud Road onto Lewis Lane.

"Darn," Beth Ann muttered. "Darn, darn, and double darn."

"What?" Megan jumped to her feet. "What is it?"

Beth Ann's lips thinned. "Kaitlin Kessler, that's what it is."

"Kessler? As in the Kessler Boulevard Kesslers?"

"None other. Kaitlin's the last of the oldest family of McCray County. I thought she was gone for good. I certainly did hope so."

Megan was a bit taken aback by Beth Ann's vehemence. "Why? Is she a troublemaker?"

Beth Ann grimaced, then shrugged. "I may as well tell you. You'd hear anyway."

"Hear? Hear what?"

"That Daniel and Kaitlin were once engaged. I figure they would be married now except Kaitlin declared she couldn't be happy living in McCray County. She moved to California about two years ago and assured everyone it was for good. I wonder what she meant when she said she was back?"

"Does she have relatives here she can visit?"

"Nope. She doesn't even have any close friends around here that I know of. Except Daniel of course. Uh oh! I'll bet the only reason she was driving down Redbud Road was to see if Daniel was at home."

Megan didn't understand why her stomach was dropping so fast. She was attracted to Daniel, of course. But surely physical attraction didn't result in the emotions that were sweeping her now.

Unless it was an unusually strong attraction. An attraction such as she felt toward Daniel. And he seemingly felt for her.

Perhaps it was best that Kaitlin Kessler was back in town. The last thing Megan needed was to fall in love with a county sheriff who disapproved of her family, her wardrobe, and her lifestyle.

Yes. Falling in love was absolutely the very last thing she needed. After all, in less than three weeks, she would be driving out of McCray County for good. She would put the whole incident behind her, except for her friendship with Beth Ann and Trevor and a few of the other wonderful citizens of McCray County.

She wouldn't want to lose touch with the judge or Miss Evelyn or . . . Wait! She mustn't think about those things now. Tears were building behind her eyes and she refused to cry any more this afternoon. Beth Ann might assume she was upset because Daniel's old girlfriend was back in town and that wasn't the case.

Not at all.

Absolutely not.

She could care less that Kaitlin Kessler was back in town. Kaitlin with the glossy blond hair and the bright red car. Kaitlin with the sophistication of having lived in California for two years. Kaitlin with the McCray County pedigree that went back further than Daniel's!

"Megan?" Beth Ann laid a hand on Megan's shoulder. "Are you okay?"

Megan squared her shoulders. "I'm fine. I'm fabulous." She spotted Daniel's car turning onto Redbud Road. "I'm also famished. Let's go inside and fix supper."

Beth Ann's gaze swept from the patrol car to Megan's face and back again. "Inside," she repeated. "Absolutely! Let's go inside right now." She hurried over to the screen door and opened it for Megan. "After you, my friend. After you!"

As soon as Megan swept past her, Beth Ann turned back to gaze for a second at the house across the street. A bright red Jaguar pulled off of Lewis Lane onto Redbud Road and eased up next to the curb in front of Daniel's house. A slender figure exited the car and hurried down the driveway toward the back of the house where Daniel had parked. Beth Ann stepped inside and eased the screen door closed behind her.

The following day being Saturday with no tutoring session scheduled, Megan had intended to spend the day cleaning Beth Ann's house. She thought it was the least she could do, considering how kind Beth Ann had been. But then Beth Ann had asked her to help out in the store, and she had of course said yes, especially after Beth Ann explained that Saturday was her busiest day and she was really hoping to make a little extra profit today so she could buy Trevor the pair of athletic shoes he had been wanting.

They stopped by the diner for a quick breakfast, and Megan was delighted to see that the town was unusually busy. Surely some of the crowd would stop by Beth Ann's store and shop. Megan had made it a point to wear only clothing that she had bought from Beth Ann. After all, she hoped to serve as a walking advertisement for her dear friend.

By 10:00, when Beth Ann flipped the sign in the shop window from CLOSED to OPEN, Megan had had a crash course in how to operate the cash register and the credit card reader. She was a little nervous, but at the same time she looked forward to the day.

Within a half-hour, she had discovered that she had a natural affinity for selling clothes. At least three ladies asked for her advice and ended up buying outfits they would never have considered otherwise. And two others decided to buy the exact ensemble that Megan had chosen to wear.

By noon, when business slowed a little, Megan was more than ready to get off her feet for a while. She was also more than a little hungry. She turned to Beth Ann. "Want me to go to the diner and bring us back some lunch?"

"Great idea," Beth Ann replied. "I don't want to close and run a chance of missing business. Get me a burger and . . ."

The tiny bell over the front door jingled and both women turned to look.

"Hi Daniel," Beth Ann called out. "What can we do for you today?"

"I thought you lovely ladies might agree to let me treat you to lunch at the diner."

"Good timing," Beth Ann said. "Megan was just headed that way, but I'm eating in today."

"Yes, you are," Megan agreed, "but not by yourself." She turned to Daniel. "I'm getting our lunch and bringing it back here to eat."

"In that case, why don't I go get lunch for all three of us and . . ."

The bell over the front door jingled again. Three heads turned to check out the new arrival.

Kaitlin Kessler stepped inside and paused to push her sunglasses to the top of her head. Her yellow sundress was cut low in the back, and her brown sandals and handbag provided a nice contrast. When she smiled, she looked directly toward Daniel.

"Why hello again, Dan, my man. I was surprised to see you heading into Beth Ann's little dress shop. Are you looking for something for your momma for her birthday? She was born on June 19, wasn't she?"

Megan glanced at Daniel. His jaw had set and a slight flush touched his face. Something was obviously going on here. She had no idea what it could be, so she listened closely to Daniel's reply.

"Hi Kait. No, my mother wasn't born until July 29. I'm visiting with my friends here. You know Beth Ann. Have you met Miss Marsh?"

Kaitlin tipped her head to one side. "Not officially, I'm afraid, but I've heard just skads about her, of course. Everyone in town is talking about the Magnificent Miss Marsh."

Megan suppressed a smile, even as she noticed a quick frown settling on Beth Ann's brow. Megan had caught the underlying tone of disapproval in Kaitlin's voice and recognized it for what it was. Kaitlin resented anyone besides herself being the center of attention in McCray County.

"Why thank you, Miss Kessler," Megan said. She had learned long ago how to deal with women who tried to put her down. "You're so very kind."

Kaitlin lifted her chin a notch. "Not nearly so kind as you, apparently. I hear nothing but praise for your generosity in tutoring our county's children. You're an out-of-work schoolteacher, I assume."

"At the moment, yes." Megan smiled. "But teachers are in such demand these days, I suspect I'll find something before this fall."

"And where might you be applying?"

Beth Ann stepped forward. "She might be applying right here in McCray County if she wanted to. I've heard more than one person say she would be a wonderful addition to our school system."

Kaitlin glanced at Beth Ann but quickly turned her attention back to Megan. "I hear you're related to the Marsh family of Atlanta." She dropped her gaze to Megan's feet, shod in an inexpensive pair of sandals from Beth Ann's shop, then slowly took in Megan's coordinated cotton slacks and blouse. "I find that hard to believe."

"Then I won't try to convince you otherwise." Megan's smile widened. "Can we help you with some shopping today?"

"Heavens no." Kaitlin effected a slight shudder. "I just followed Dan in here. His father is looking for him." She turned to Daniel. "I ran into your father at the diner, Dan, and he asked me to let you know that old Mr. Millsaps called in a complaint about tourists bothering his bull again."

Daniel's lips thinned, then he shrugged and nodded. "I'd better drive out his way and check the fence along Highway Two-twenty-seven. I've yet to find any indication that someone's pestering that bull, but I can't convince Marvin Millsaps of that."

He glanced at Megan but immediately turned his gaze to Beth Ann. "Sorry about lunch." He glanced at Megan again. "Maybe another time."

Beth Ann cocked her head to one side and grinned. "I would say 'bull' but it's actually appropriate in this case."

Kaitlin groaned. "Oh for heaven's sake, Beth Ann, I see that you haven't matured an iota since high school." She placed a hand on Daniel's arm. "Shall I tell your daddy you've gone to check on the problem, Dan?"

He took a quick step toward the door, dislodging Kaitlin's hand. "Fine." He quickened his stride. "I'll see you ladies later."

"Wait, Dan." Kaitlin hurried after him. "I'm sure your father was hoping you'd take time for lunch. Let's go to the—"

The door shut behind them, cutting off Kaitlin's last word, but Megan completed the sentence for her. "Diner. Do you suppose Daniel will actually fall for that blatant attempt to manipulate him?"

"Let's see." Beth Ann made a dash for the door and peeked out. "Nope. He's managed to shake her off and he's getting into the patrol car."

"In that case," Megan said, "I'll go on to the diner and pick up our lunch."

"You might as well. Kaitlin's not going back to

the diner. In fact, she's getting in her car and heading out of town. Surely to goodness she's not going to follow Daniel."

Megan shrugged. "Who knows? I'm merely interested in lunch right now. What do you want?"

She jotted down Beth Ann's order, all the while studiously ignoring the slight smile pulling at the corners of her friend's lips.

Chapter Nine

By the time they closed the shop Saturday evening, both Beth Ann and Megan were delighted. Beth Ann's profits that day meant she could buy Trevor the athletic shoes he had been wanting and also bank a couple of hundred dollars to go toward the $2,000 roofing job her house had been needing for the past six months.

Exhausted, the two had come home, kicked off their shoes, collapsed in a couple of overstuffed chairs in the parlor, and were actively ignoring Trevor's frequent demands to know what they had planned for supper.

"Go away, little boy," Beth Ann muttered, making Trevor giggle.

"You're my momma, you can't send me away," he informed her.

"Don't remind me."

"I won't if you'll give me money to go to the diner for supper."

"Sonny was closing early tonight, remember? His nephew's getting married in Suttertown."

Megan slumped further into her chair. "I'll fix some supper if someone can help me to the kitchen. I don't think I can make it under my own power."

"I'll help . . . ," Trevor said, then paused and listened for a second. "Did I hear somebody at the door?"

"Don't know," Beth Ann said. "Why don't you check?"

A voice sounded from the rear of the house. "Hello? Anybody home?"

"It's Sheriff McCray!" Trevor yelled before making a mad dash for the back door.

Fatigue forgotten, Megan pushed herself upright in the chair and reached to straighten her hair. She had barely finished when Daniel and Trevor entered the room. Trevor ran to his mother's side.

"Sheriff McCray's invited us over for supper, Mom. I'm starving, and you're too tired to cook. Can we go, please?"

Megan watched Daniel, who had stopped by Beth Ann's chair. "Yeah, Mom," Daniel said, grinning. "Please? I'm working on my barbecue and ice cream recipes for the Fourth festivities, and I need tasters."

He turned to Megan. "You're needed too, Miss Marsh. The more critics I have now, the better my chances on the Fourth."

"Chances for what?"

"Has no one told you about our Fourth of July celebration? It's a major county occasion, and prizes are offered for the best barbecue and the best homemade ice cream. I enter every year, but Uncle Bob always wins. This year I have a couple of new recipes and I'm hoping to tromp him into the ground."

"An admirable ambition," Megan said. "I'd be delighted to help."

"Me too, me too. I love homemade ice cream." Trevor jumped up and down. "Can we go, Mom? I mean, *may* we go?"

"Since you're using correct grammar, I don't see how I can say no," Beth Ann said. "And I wouldn't mind a little homemade barbecue and ice cream myself. What kind of ice cream, Daniel?"

"Strawberry. I picked the berries myself and put them in the freezer. This ice cream is going to taste like fresh out-of-the-patch strawberries."

Beth Ann stood and struck a pose. "Then move

aside, peons, and make way for the queen of the strawberry festival." She reached up to straighten an imaginary crown, then twirled an imaginary cape, and strutted from the room. A giggling Trevor fell in behind, then stooped to grab and carry her imaginary train. Megan and Daniel were left behind in the parlor.

"What is that all about?" Megan asked, nodding toward Trevor's retreating back as she started to follow him. Daniel fell into step beside her.

"When Beth Ann and I were teenagers, the town had a strawberry festival every spring, complete with a parade, floats, and, obviously, a queen. Beth Ann was named queen our junior year in high school. She's still trying to live it down."

"Sounds like an honor to me."

"It was, except for that red hair of hers. To tease her, everybody claimed it was her resemblance to the strawberry that earned her the crown."

"And this didn't hurt her feelings?"

"I don't think so. Beth Ann was pretty secure about who she was, even when we were teenagers. And it didn't hurt that the captain of the football team was madly in love with her and her with him."

"Trevor's dad?"

"Yep. It was rough on Beth Ann losing him so soon after they were married. She's got a lot of courage, that girl."

They had reached Daniel's yard by this time, and Trevor dashed back to join them. "The grill is smoking a lot, Sheriff McCray. Are you sure you aren't burning the ribs the way you burned the steaks when Miss Megan ate with you?"

Daniel heaved a heavy sigh, drew his eyebrows down in a feigned frown, and glared at Megan. "Just couldn't keep that as our little secret, could you?"

Megan threw up her hands. "Hey, I only told a couple of people. Is it my fault that word spreads fast in a small town?"

A different voice sounded from the gate. "Miss Marsh is certainly right about word spreading fast, Dan, my man. I heard you were looking for tasters and I came to volunteer my services."

The growl emanating from Beth Ann's direction echoed Megan's feelings toward this latest addition to the backyard barbecue. Nor did it escape her attention that Daniel hesitated for several seconds before inviting Kaitlin Kessler to join them. His tone was polite but a bit on the cool side. If Megan wasn't badly mistaken, he was no happier to see Kaitlin than the rest of the small backyard party.

If Kaitlin was aware of her lack of welcome, she apparently didn't care. She hurried to Daniel's side, took his arm, and struck up a conversation in such low tones that no one else could join in.

Megan drifted toward the side of the yard where a yew hedge separated the backyard from the street. A few seconds later, Beth Ann joined her, but immediately Trevor yelled for his mom to come see the toad he had discovered hiding inside one of the concrete urns decorating the patio.

"I'd better go," Beth Ann muttered. "If I don't, he'll grab the toad and bring it to me. Excuse me, Meg. I'll be back in a minute."

Megan laughed. "No problem, Beth Ann. Better that you should go to the toad than that the toad should be brought to us."

Beth Ann muttered something under her breath about aggravating little boys and hurried away. Megan pulled a deep breath into her lungs. The delightful fragrance of homemade barbecue had drifted from the grill to the side of the yard. Megan's stomach growled rather loudly.

But where had that whimper come from? Surely her stomach had not made that sound.

Megan shifted slightly, just enough to give her a sideways view of the hedge, and was not surprised to see a couple of eyes staring into the backyard. They were filled with so much longing, Megan was hard pressed not to whimper herself.

As she watched, a grubby little hand came up to part the hedge just a bit more, and a small face pressed closer through the greenery.

Megan forced a sigh, then spoke softly. "Hi there. No, don't run away. I need your help."

The little boy, who had quickly withdrawn when Megan spoke, paused, then pressed his face back into the hole he had formed with his hands.

"What kind of help?"

"I'm feeling a little bit left out here. I'm a stranger in town, and everybody at this cookout has known each other forever. I'd sure appreciate it if you'd join me. You could be my friend and I wouldn't feel like such an outsider."

"Hey lady, this is Sheriff McCray's place. Since you're a stranger, maybe you don't know that he's forever throwing my daddy in jail for being drunk. I don't think he'd want me to eat with you folks." He licked his lips and stared at the ice cream churn sitting in the corner of the patio. "I hate not to be your friend, though."

"Don't worry about the sheriff. I'll explain that you're my guest. He won't mind. Go around to the gate and I'll meet you there."

Megan glanced toward Daniel. Kaitlin still pressed as close to his side as she could manage without falling into the grill. And Beth Ann was apparently in deep admiration of the toad Trevor had unearthed. Megan hurried to open the gate.

The little boy who stepped inside was thin almost to the point of appearing frail. His dirty jeans were several inches too short, and his skin showed through his worn tee in half a dozen places.

Megan smiled. "Thank you so much for helping me out. Maybe you'd better tell me your name before we join the others."

He stared at the ground. "I'm Mikie."

"Hi Mikie. My name is Megan but Trevor calls me 'Miss Megan.'"

"All right then, I'll call you Miss Megan too. Am I really invited for supper?"

"Absolutely. Come on, let's find out what's on the menu besides barbecue and ice cream."

She reached for his grimy hand and pulled the little boy along beside her toward the grill.

"Hey Daniel," she called. "I've lined up another taster for you."

Daniel looked around. A flicker of surprise touched his face, followed quickly by a wide smile. "Hello, Mikie. It sure is brave of you to help us out tonight. It takes a lot of courage to serve as one of my tasters."

Megan glanced at Kaitlin, who made no effort to hide her disgust. Fortunately Trevor had spotted the little boy and ran to greet him.

"Hey, Mikie. Want to see the toad I found?"

Mikie glanced at Megan, who smiled and nodded. "Go with Trevor if you want. I'll be sure to call you when supper's ready."

"Okay then." He turned and followed Trevor in

a dead run back to the patio. A second later, Beth Ann joined Megan. "Thanks for the rescue," she murmured, then turned to Daniel. "Say, Daniel, couldn't we be of some assistance? No sense in you having to do everything."

"Thanks, Beth Ann. The ribs are about ready, so you ladies can carry the slaw and baked beans out of the kitchen onto the screened-in porch and set a couple of extra places at the table."

"Want to help, Kaitlin?" Beth Ann called.

"No thanks, Beth, honey. You gals don't need me. I'll stay here in case Daniel needs any assistance."

"I've got this, Kaitlin. Why don't you go tell the boys it's time to wash up."

Kaitlin's lips formed a grimace of distaste, but she hesitated for only a second before walking toward the patio. A few seconds later, her scream tore through the quiet of the evening.

Daniel, who had just lifted the last rack of ribs off the grill, dropped his tongs and ran toward the patio. Megan and Beth Ann arrived only seconds behind him.

Kaitlin, her face flushed with fury, clutched her arm halfway between her elbow and wrist.

Daniel stopped beside her. "What is it, Kaitlin? Did you get stung? What's wrong with your arm?"

"Those boys, those hideous little boys, they did this. They flung a nasty, slimy, ugly toad on me."

"A toad?" Daniel echoed. "That's all? You aren't hurt then?"

"Of course I'm hurt. Can't you see I'm terrified? I'm going to murder those little heathens."

Megan turned to look for Mikie, only to see him slipping back through the hedge. Trevor clung to his mother, half hiding behind her. He cringed when Beth Ann stepped to one side, grabbed him by the arm, and drew him forward. "What do you have to say about this, young man?"

"It was an accident, Mom, I swear. I was holding the toad and when I opened my hand to show it to Miss Kessler, it hopped onto her arm. I didn't mean for it to jump."

"And you didn't throw it on Miss Kessler?" Daniel asked.

"No, Sheriff McCray." Trevor gulped. "And Mikie never even touched the toad so Miss Kessler ought not to have called him a heathen."

"No," Daniel said solemnly. "She ought not, and I'm sure she'd like to apologize to him." He glanced around the backyard. "Where is Mikie?"

Megan stepped forward. "He left when Miss Kessler threatened to murder him."

Kaitlin twirled to glare at Megan. "This is all your fault, dragging that little piece of trash into our company. His daddy is the town drunk, a bum, and as worthless as they come. That type doesn't belong with polite society."

Megan lifted her chin. "I'm not sure you would recognize *polite* society if you encountered it, Miss Kessler."

Kaitlin turned to Daniel. "I'm sorry, Dan, but if you're going to associate with the lower classes, I don't believe I can justify staying for supper."

Daniel nodded. "I think you're absolutely right, Kaitlin. You should go. Good-bye."

Kaitlin glared at Daniel with a curled lip. "You'll never change. You were a pathetic small-town rube when I left you two years ago, and you're even more pathetic now. I'm going back to California where people understand that there's nothing wrong with having a little fun instead of always trying to live up to some inane and outdated sense of duty. Good-bye." Kaitlin grabbed her purse and stalked through the grass, slamming the garden gate behind her.

"Well," Beth Ann drawled, "as Great Aunt Brenda would have said, good riddance to bad rubbish."

"Amen," Daniel said. "But I'm sorry she ran little Mikie Smith off before she left."

"Let's find him," Megan said. "He was hungry and he was looking forward to supper. Where could he have gone, Daniel?"

Trevor stepped forward. "I think I know. He might have gone to the library. Mikie spends a lot of time there."

"How do you know?" Beth Ann asked.

"All the kids know that, Mom. Mikie don't like to go home, so he hangs out in the library looking at picture books. He doesn't read very good but he pretends he can so that the librarian won't kick him out."

"What about his mother?" Megan asked.

"She died soon after Mikie was born," Daniel responded. "I doubt he remembers her."

Megan pressed a hand against her stomach. "That poor child. I wish I could get him into my tutoring class."

"He'd like that, I think," Trevor said. "But he won't come because his clothes are so ratty."

"Well, my gosh," Beth Ann said. "We could fix that. He's about a size behind you, so we could outfit him in some of the clothes you grew out of while they were still good."

"I could buy him some new clothes," Megan interjected.

"Whoa, ladies, I'm afraid you're getting ahead of yourselves. Mikie would have to square most of these plans with his dad before we could proceed, but we could at least feed him supper tonight if we can find him."

A second later, Mikie stepped around the corner of the house. "I'm past ready for supper," he said, looking straight at Daniel before turning to Megan. "And fancy clothes or not, Miss Megan, I'd sure love to be tutored to read. If I could read good, I could move from the little kids' section of the library into the young people's section. I'd like that a lot."

Megan blinked rapidly, then smiled. "I'd like that a lot too, Mikie. Now let's eat and then we'll talk about you joining my tutoring group on Monday."

Chapter Ten

At 9:00 on Monday morning, a knock sounded on Beth Ann's front door. Since Beth Ann had already left for work, Megan hurried to open the door. Standing on the front porch, hat in hand, was Daniel. Beside him was Mikie Smith, dressed in brand new jeans, sneakers, and T-shirt.

"Hi, Miss Megan," Mikie said, grinning broadly. "I'm ready to be tutored."

"That's wonderful, Mikie." Megan grinned back. "I'm as anxious to get started as you are. Why don't you step into the parlor there and be looking at the books and magazines spread out on the table. We'll choose something to work on after I've had a chance to speak to Sheriff McCray for a minute."

Megan waited until Mikie disappeared into the parlor, then she stepped onto the front porch. As usual, her heart rate accelerated when she looked into Daniel's eyes, but she forced herself to pretend that she didn't feel anything out of the ordinary and could only hope her gaze didn't give her away. "You're here bright and early this morning. Did you get permission from Mikie's dad for him to participate in the tutoring sessions?"

Daniel nodded solemnly. "I did. I dropped by the house yesterday afternoon and was fortunate enough to catch his dad almost sober. He agreed readily enough."

"And the new clothes?"

"Mikie has agreed to help me out in the yard a bit this summer—raking, weeding the flowers, things like that. As a bit of advance on his pay, we stopped by Arnold's Store and I let him pick out a few things he liked."

Megan laid a hand on Daniel's arm. "What a wonderful thing to do for Mikie. You kept him from having to settle for either hand-me-downs or charity. Your thoughtfulness humbles me."

"And yours shames me. I should have seen that Mikie was in need without someone from outside the county bringing it to my attention."

Megan dropped her hand. She was amazed at the sudden surge of hurt that twisted her heart merely because Daniel had called her an outsider.

He hadn't meant to be cruel. He was merely stating facts. So why did she have to struggle to keep tears from forming? She turned and grasped the screen door handle. "I'd better get inside and work with Mikie a few minutes before the other children get here."

"Okay, but I have a favor to ask of you. After your tutoring session today, would you bring Mikie by my house? I'm taking the day off to get some chores lined up for him, but before he starts working, I'd like to take both of you out to lunch."

"I'll be glad to bring him by, but you don't have to buy lunch for me."

"Sure I do. Mikie'll be much more comfortable with you along, and I'm going to make sure he gets at least one decent meal a day while he's working for me."

"When you put it that way, of course I'll come." And because she didn't want Daniel to read the eagerness in her eyes, she quickly stepped inside and closed the screen door behind her.

Megan soon discovered that Mikie read far below grade level, but she had expected that. She also knew that because he was highly motivated to learn, she had a very good chance to help him move ahead by at least two grade levels before her community service was over.

More and more, she found herself dreading the

end of her time in McCray County. She adored
Beth Ann and Trevor, of course, and she was fond
of the children in her group, but more than that,
she felt a strong tie to Daniel that she didn't fully
understand. She couldn't deny that there was
something between them that she had never experienced before.

And because she couldn't stop looking forward
to lunch with Daniel, the morning seemed to drag,
even though the youngsters were well behaved,
and warmly welcomed Mikie into their midst.

But finally the old grandfather clock in the
hallway chimed 11:30, and Megan instructed her
students to put away their books. By 11:45, she
was leading Mikie across the street to Daniel's
house.

Mikie paused as soon as they had stepped onto
the sidewalk that led to Daniel's front porch. "Do
you suppose the sheriff will let me feed
Eisenhower?"

Megan paused too. "I wouldn't get my hopes
up, Mikie. Eisenhower is extremely shy. I've only
seen him once, and I'm staying across the street."

Mikie sighed. "I like cats. Maybe he'll know I
like cats and will let me pet him sometime."

"I suspect he will, but you'll have to be patient."

"It's hard being patient sometimes, but I know
how."

"I'm sure you do, Mikie. And I sincerely

believe you'll be rewarded some day for being such a patient young man."

Mikie's face brightened. "You think so, Miss Megan?"

"I do, Mikie. I surely do."

"Do you think if I'm really patient and good, you might keep on teaching me to read, even after the summer's over?"

"Oh Mikie, I would love nothing better, but I'll be leaving McCray County in a couple of weeks."

"Why?"

"Well, I, eh . . . oh, there's Daniel coming through the garden gate. I'll bet he's looking for us."

Daniel stepped onto the sideway. "You'd be right, Miss Megan. I was beginning to think you and Mikie had gotten lost on your way across the street."

Mikie laughed. "We're not that silly, Sheriff. I was just talking to Miss Megan about her staying in McCray County."

Daniel's gaze cut to Megan. "And what was she saying to you in return?"

"She's going away pretty soon. I'm sure sorry."

"Me too, Mikie. Me too." Daniel looked into Megan's eyes, and his expression was so solemn and so sad, Megan felt her heart rate increase. She wrenched her gaze away and looked down at the little boy beside her.

"Mikie and I are pretty hungry, Sheriff. Do I

recall you mentioning that you were going to buy us some lunch?"

"Would a picnic in my backyard be an agreeable substitute?"

"Yeah," Mikie said with a wide grin. "With sandwiches and cake and lemonade?"

"I've got the sandwiches and lemonade, but you'll have to settle for cold watermelon instead of cake."

Mikie's eyes widened. "Watermelon? Is that one covered in ice in that tub over there?" He licked his lips. "I ain't had no watermelon in ages."

Megan looked at Daniel, who was looking back with a half-smile and a question in his eyes. Was Megan going to correct Mikie's grammar?

She smiled back and shrugged. "Me neither," she said, eliciting a grin from Daniel. "That'll be great. Can I help in some way?"

"Sure. Everything's in the kitchen, ready to carry out to the patio. Since I'm taking today off, I used my morning to prepare our lunch." He motioned toward the glass-topped table on the patio, where the centerpiece was a bunch of daisies stuck in a quart canning jar. Bright red napkins and green paper placemats were already in place.

Mikie had run ahead to the patio, and Megan allowed Daniel to take her hand and walk with her toward the kitchen door. How on earth, she wondered, had Daniel gone so long without being snatched up by some local female? He was surely everything a McCray County woman could want in a husband. Not only was he handsome, he was also gentle, kind, compassionate, and handy in the kitchen. If only she weren't—

"After you," Daniel said, opening the kitchen door and motioning Megan in ahead of him. She was greeted by a jumble of odors, from the tart fragrance of fresh lemons to the more robust smells of mustard and pickles.

Megan could judge immediately that the kitchen had been modernized. A large stainless steel refrigerator stood against the wall to her left, and a matching range was located to her right. A window above the stainless steel sink looked out on the backyard, and a small wooden table stood against the far wall.

Daniel motioned toward the table. "The lemonade's in that pitcher. If you'll take it out to the patio, I'll get the sandwich makings out of the refrigerator and then come back for the condiments."

"I can take those too." Megan reached for the handle of the restaurant-type rack holding containers of mustard, mayo, and a jar of pickles.

"Let me get the door for you then."

Megan nodded. "Nice kitchen."

"Thanks. Beth Ann probably told you this house belonged to my grandfather."

"Yes, she did. Do you like living here?"

"I love it. I love the character of older houses."

"I do too. My grandmother on my father's side had a house similar to this in Atlanta. It was razed and replaced by an office building when I was about ten."

"That's too bad."

"Yes, but my father and his brothers were all married and had their own homes by that time. None of them wanted to be saddled with a house that they wouldn't be living in."

The door opened and Mikie stuck his head in the kitchen. "Hey, Sheriff McCray, I think I saw Eisenhower hiding behind that big oak near the fence. Can I try to pet him?"

Daniel turned to the little boy. "Not yet, Mikie. Wait until he comes to you. He'll get used to you being around in a few days and then he'll make the first move. Try to be patient until then."

"I will, Sheriff. And I'm being patient about lunch too, even though I'm pretty hungry."

Daniel laughed. "Come in and wash your hands, then. By the time you finish, Miss Megan and I will have the picnic makings outside."

"Whew!" Mikie breathed a sigh of relief and hurried toward the washroom Daniel pointed out to him. Megan grabbed the pitcher and condiments and headed for the back door, pausing only to allow Daniel to open the door for her.

She hurried outside and quickly placed the lemonade and condiments on the table, then stepped off the patio and paused under the shade of a huge maple. She needed a second to shake off the longings that had inundated her in Daniel's kitchen. A simple life with a man like Daniel . . . the thought was so appealing, Megan could almost forget that she had already mapped out her future.

She blew her breath out in a long sigh. Every moment she spent in this man's company endeared him to her more, but she was going to be leaving McCray County in less than a month. She'd better be careful about how much she became attached to Daniel McCray.

"Miss Megan!" Mikie hurried over to grasp her hand. "Come on. Our picnic's ready. Aren't you hungry?"

Megan looked toward Daniel, who was watching her with an expression of concern in his eyes. She forced a smile and allowed Mikie to pull her toward the patio. "I'm definitely ready for some lunch," she declared, then lifted the pitcher and poured lemonade in plastic glasses while Daniel uncovered the bread and luncheon meats.

Forty-five minutes later, after each of them had polished off a couple of sandwiches and a slice of cold watermelon, Daniel asked Megan to wait at the table while he escorted Mikie to a flower bed at the back of the lot and set him to pulling weeds. He then returned to sit across the table from Megan where he could look directly into her eyes.

"I'd like to ask you a very personal question," he said.

Megan nodded. "Okay."

"You told me once that you had goals that couldn't be accomplished in the country. What did you mean by that?"

Megan took a deep breath. "Long story, but I'll make it as succinct as possible. My mother had always wanted to be an inner city teacher. She related to children especially well, and she thought she could make a difference in the lives of children who did not have idyllic childhoods. She had planned to start her teaching career in the fall after she and my father married in June. Then she discovered she was pregnant with me."

"So she delayed her plans?"

"Yes, she decided to wait until I was five and had entered kindergarten before she started teaching. When I was five, she learned she had cancer. She fought it for three years, but she lost the battle when I was eight. Her dream to make a difference for those children became my dream. I not only trained to become a teacher with a specialty in reading, but I also took specialized training for urban settings. I don't want to let that go to waste."

"You told me you had a disagreement with your father. Does he object to your plans?"

"He's afraid for me, and I understand that, but he went too far in his efforts to protect me. He used his influence in Atlanta to keep me from getting an interview for the job I wanted. I left home immediately and was headed for Chicago when Deputy Barnhart pulled me over. I was hoping my Uncles D would help me get a job in an urban school there."

"So when Uncle Bob sentenced you to community service on trumped-up charges, you accepted because you wanted to prove to yourself that you could cope with a difficult situation?"

"Exactly. And frankly, the experience has done a lot for my self-confidence."

"It's been good for me too. You've helped me see that not all young women with plenty of money are like Kaitlin Kessler."

Megan grimaced. "I would hope not. Frankly, I'm surprised you were ever involved with a woman like her."

"She wasn't so jaded when we were in high school. In fact, she was a very sweet girl who wanted the same things I wanted—a life here in McCray County where we could raise a family and try to instill the same values in our children that our parents had instilled in us. It was only after Kaitlin went away to college that her goals changed. Suddenly she wanted to be famous and envied for her possessions and her beauty."

"I feel sorry for her in a way."

"You would. You're that kind of person. Which makes me hope that you won't turn down the proposition I have for you."

"Proposition?"

"There are a lot of youngsters similar to Mikie in McCray County. The poverty level is high, and a lot of parents lose hope and then try to shake their sense of hopelessness through drug use or alcohol. I'd like to recruit some of those children to join your tutoring session if you're willing to stretch it out a bit."

Megan shook her head. "That's a wonderful idea, but I don't have time. I wouldn't want to attempt something like that in less than six weeks, and I'll be leaving McCray County in less than a month."

"You could stay until the middle of July instead of leaving at the end of June."

"But then I wouldn't have a chance to find a teaching position for the fall. I'm sorry, Daniel, but I just can't see how I could extend my session, and I feel badly because your idea was incredibly kind and generous."

He ducked his head. "Don't give me too much credit, Megan. I had an ulterior motive."

He looked up, directly into her eyes, and his gaze was filled with such longing, Megan felt an ache growing inside her. She moistened her lips. "What do you mean?"

"I was hoping to spend more time with you. What's between us—however one might define that phenomenal attraction—it isn't going away, and I've got a feeling even the distance between here and Chicago won't weaken its effects, at least for me."

Megan sighed. "I wish things were different, Daniel. But you belong here in McCray County, and I belong in a city. Whatever we may feel toward each other doesn't change that."

"Maybe not. But denying our feelings doesn't seem right either."

"I agree. But what else can we do?"

"You could use my computer and try to apply for a teaching position in Chicago online. That would give you a couple more weeks here, a couple more weeks when we could work together toward helping some of the less fortunate children in McCray County and see where our feelings take us. I don't know about you, but I need to know whether this thing between us is real or some summer enchantment."

Megan nodded. "Good idea. I'll get online this

afternoon if your computer's free. When can you start lining up more students?"

"I'll start working on it this afternoon. Why don't we meet back here around seven and compare notes?"

Megan stood. "See you at seven."

Chapter Eleven

Long before 7:00 that evening, Megan had visited the website of the Chicago Public Schools and entered her teaching application online. She had also called her Uncle Dayton on her cell phone and asked him to send her some information on housing in Chicago.

Still, the sense of accomplishment she had expected to feel did not materialize. She might be a step closer to realizing her dream, but what she really looked forward to was spending an additional two weeks in McCray County.

A bit irritated with herself, she shut down Daniel's computer, let herself out his back door, and hurried across the street to begin preparing for tomorrow's tutoring session. If she was going to

take on additional children, she needed to check
her supplies and invest in some additional books
and magazines.

After completing the inventory, she took her
pad and settled down in the glider on Beth Ann's
front porch to work on the list of the materials she
needed. She didn't notice Beth Ann approaching
until her friend greeted her from the top step.

"Hey Meg, what are you doing?"

"Good heavens! Is it five-thirty already?"

Beth Ann stepped onto the porch, then dropped
into a wicker chair. "More like a quarter 'til six. I
got held up when Mrs. Dalton came in five minutes before closing time. But I can't complain. At
least she bought a pair of shorts and a top. How's
your day been?"

"I applied for a teaching job online."

"Where?"

"Chicago."

Beth Ann grimaced. "You're really going to
leave us, aren't you?"

"Not immediately. Daniel talked me into spending a couple more weeks here and expanding my
tutoring session—if that's okay by you, of
course."

Beth Ann's eyes brightened. "You know it's fine
with me. I never want to see you leave. But tell me
more about this expanded tutoring session. Who
are the other students?"

"I don't know yet. Daniel's working on setting it up now. We're meeting at seven at his house to compare notes."

"Ah!" Beth Ann ducked her head but not in time to hide a knowing smile.

"It's purely business," Megan declared.

"Sure it is, honey, sure it is!" Beth Ann jumped to her feet. "I think I'll change clothes and see if I can round up my son. He's been pestering me to have dinner at the diner, and I believe I'll take him tonight."

Megan raised her brows. "Excuse me, but I can't help wondering, Beth Ann. Why are you suddenly taking Trevor out tonight when you've been refusing for the past week?"

Beth Ann grinned, then shrugged. "You're a smart lady, Megan Marsh. You figure it out." She pulled the screen door open and disappeared inside the house.

Half an hour later, Megan had the house to herself again. Beth Ann and Trevor had waved on their way out the door but neither had paused for conversation. Megan decided to grab a quick shower before meeting with Daniel.

Then, for reasons she preferred not to examine too closely, she picked out an outfit that had been in her suitcase the day Horace pulled her over—a deceptively simple white cotton sleeveless dress with lace around the hem, and white sandals accented with tiny white flowers. Although the dress wasn't especially revealing, it did cling to her curves in ways that attested to the talents of its renowned designer.

Before she could change her mind, Megan let herself out the side door and hurried across the street.

Daniel answered her knock at the front door, then grasped the edge of the door and gulped. "If you don't mind my saying so, wow!"

Megan smiled. "I felt like dressing up a bit this evening. Looks as though I'm not the only one." She nodded toward Daniel's crisp dark jeans, white shirt, and tan jacket.

"I'm hoping I can talk you into going out to dinner. There's a nice restaurant in Smithwood, which is only about twenty miles from here. How about it?"

"I'd love to."

"Great! I've already pulled the car around." He nodded toward a bright red, fully restored 1969 Mustang sitting next to the curb in front of the house.

Megan regarded the sparkling car with widened eyes. "As you so recently and eloquently stated: Wow! But why haven't I seen this beautiful vintage vehicle before?"

"I keep it in the detached garage on the far side

of the house and bring it out only for special occasions, like tonight."

Megan grinned. "Quite the charmer, aren't you, Mr. McCray?"

Daniel grinned back. "My daddy always told me that the way to a girl's heart was through a shiny car."

"He did not! Your father is too much a gentleman to tell you any such thing."

"Zounds! Foiled again!" Daniel twirled an imaginary mustache, then laughed before offering Megan his arm and leading her down the porch steps and out to the front curb.

Daniel helped Megan into the passenger's seat and closed the door, then started around the back of the car. Megan leaned back into the luxurious upholstery and closed her eyes. This night, she instinctively understood, was going to be wonderful. Being alone with Daniel in the intimate confines of an old car smelling of rich leather, the soft night air caressing her skin. This, she realized, was a way of life she could enjoy for the rest of her days.

Startled, she immediately opened her eyes. She mustn't forget her dream. She had wanted to be an inner city teacher ever since she could remember. That had been her mother's dream, and it had become hers too. It was what she wanted most in the world.

Then Daniel settled himself behind the steering wheel and turned the key in the ignition. The engine started with a sedate purr, and Megan smiled to herself. She would not forsake her dream, but that didn't mean she couldn't enjoy tonight and the next few weeks. Nor did it mean that she shouldn't treat herself to the pleasure of spending time in the company of this man she liked so much.

By the time dinner ended that evening, Megan knew she was falling in love with Daniel. They had laughed together, shared stories about their childhoods, and thoroughly discussed their individual likes and dislikes where food was concerned. Daniel, she had discovered, detested seafood, possibly because he had been raised so far inland, while Megan was certain she could live on shrimp and lobster.

Overall, they shared the same tastes in music and movies although not in novels. Megan, by virtue of her training, was widely read in adolescent literature and current periodicals, while Daniel preferred history and mysteries.

The ride home along sparsely traveled highways lined with old growth forests was far more enchanting for Megan than she would have believed possible. She had been born and raised near Atlanta, and she would have sworn that the sprawling city was in her blood. Hadn't she always dreamed of living deep in the pulsing center of such a metropolis? The sights and sounds of city life had always fascinated her. She had loved the anonymity of walking down a busy street and meeting no one who recognized her.

How could she now prefer the quiet but all-knowing life in a small town? There was no anonymity here, no way of insulating oneself from the nosy stares of neighbors.

But the neighbors could become lasting friends, she had learned, and the quietness hid a deep and steady devotion to the attributes that made a life worth living.

"You're awfully quiet," Daniel commented, turning his head to glance at her in the intimate dimness of the car. "What are you thinking about?"

Megan didn't speak for a minute. How could she answer him honestly when she didn't understand herself where her thoughts were taking her?

"Never mind," Daniel said a few seconds later. He turned his gaze back toward the road. "I understand that some things are personal."

"I was wondering how I could have come to love this place so much in such a short time."

Daniel glanced at her again, then, a few seconds later, pulled the car off the road onto a paved area designed as an overlook. "Want to get out and look down on the town of Smithwood?"

Megan nodded, then waited for Daniel to come around and open her car door for her. They would do more, she realized, than look down at the valley floor, but that was fine with her. She wanted to feel Daniel's strong arms around her. She wanted their lips to touch again. She wanted to feel the joy spreading through her that she had experienced in the past when he kissed her.

When Daniel opened the car door and offered his hand, Megan eagerly reached up to place her hand in his. She swung her legs around and stood, then allowed him to wrap an arm around her waist and lead her to the edge of the overlook.

Twinkling lights from the town below seemed to mirror the stars flickering in the vast sky about them. The cool night air smelled of tangy evergreens and musty forest floors. Megan leaned into Daniel's side when he wrapped his arm around her shoulder. "It's so beautiful that words don't really do it justice."

Daniel gently pulled her into his arms. "I want to kiss you again."

Megan smiled, then lifted a hand and laid it against his cheek. The smoothness suggested he had shaved just before he dressed for their evening together. "I'd like that too," she said.

The kiss was all Megan had expected and more. Never would she have believed that a simple kiss could transport her to such heights. She felt safe but at the same time recklessly daring. Her emotions soared into the night skies and glided smoothly toward the valley below. Everything around her was magical and invincible and the man kissing her with such depth of feeling was responsible for it all.

Megan simply couldn't imagine living her life without him. But she understood that she couldn't stay and that he wouldn't ask her to.

Daniel knew before the kiss began that he was in danger. He was falling in love with Megan Marsh and he suspected from the way she melted into his arms that she was falling for him too.

But they had no future together. He wouldn't ask her to give up her dream. She might say yes, and then someday—maybe it would be years down the road, but someday—she would feel guilty for putting her own desires above what she saw as her calling, and she would hate herself and maybe even him.

He couldn't imagine how terribly sad that day would be for both of them.

So he ended the kiss. It was the hardest thing he had ever done, but he did it. Although the evening had been magical, it was ending. His vintage red Mustang was about to turn into a pumpkin, and he couldn't do a thing to stop it.

He pulled back and looked down into Megan's

upturned face. "Guess we'd better get back to town." He suppressed a sigh. "I forget to tell you that I have four more students lined up to join your tutoring session in the morning."

Megan blinked. Her mind wasn't ready to make the leap from ecstasy to reality, but Daniel wasn't giving her a choice. She stepped back out of his arms. "You found some more students?"

"Yep. I contacted eight families. Two declined flat out, and two said they needed their boys to work on the farm all summer. I'm pleased with the four I got though. They are badly in need of tutoring."

"Okay," Megan said. She couldn't think about students at the moment. She could only think that Daniel obviously had not been as affected by their kiss as she had been. Otherwise he could not be standing there acting as though it had never happened. She felt tears building behind her eyes and bit her lip. "Then we'd better go," she said. "I'll need to be ready in the morning." She turned and hurried back to the Mustang, not waiting for Daniel to open the car door for her.

Chapter Twelve

At 8:00 the next morning, a timid knock sounded on Beth Ann's front door. Megan, who had tossed and turned most of the night wondering how she could have fallen in love with a man she couldn't build a life with, sat at the breakfast table nursing a cup of coffee. Beth Ann had left early because she was expecting a shipment of new merchandise and she didn't want to miss the deliveryman.

Megan had assumed she would have an hour to herself before her tutoring session began, but she pulled herself to her feet and made her way to the front door just as the knock was repeated, more loudly this time.

She opened the door and looked down into the

faces of four youngsters she had never seen before. Three were girls, all dressed in what Megan would have considered church clothes. Each clutched a small paper bag, and all regarded Megan with wide eyes. The fourth child, a boy with striking red hair, a thin face, and bare feet, stood with his hands jammed into his pockets and his chin thrust into the air. He spoke first.

"We's here to see that teacher. The sheriff sent us."

"Oh," Megan said. She had expected Daniel to escort the children and to introduce them to her. Obviously that wasn't going to happen, so what she had to do now was shake off her grogginess and try to make the children feel at ease.

She moistened her lips and smiled.

No one smiled back.

She pushed open the screen. "I'm the teacher. My name is Miss Megan. Won't you come in?"

The three girls glanced at each other, then at the boy. He nodded and the girls slipped sideways into the hall, then stood with their backs against the wall staring up at Megan.

"You'll have to excuse me," Megan said, "but I'm running a little behind this morning. First we need to get to know each other. Come into the breakfast room with me while I finish my coffee and you can tell me your names."

She turned and walked toward the back of the

house, praying that the children would follow. They did, although rather slowly.

When Megan stepped back into the breakfast room, she realized that all of Beth Ann's usual breakfast feast was still spread out on the table. Immediately upon entering the room, each child stopped to stare at the Danish and fruit.

"Would anyone care for some breakfast?" Megan asked.

The children looked at each other, then at the food. Finally one of the little girls, a small child with thick brown hair, nodded.

"Wonderful," Megan said. "Have a seat." She motioned to the chairs and stood by while each child clambered up to the table. "Just a second while I get us some plates from the kitchen."

Fifteen minutes later, the children had polished off half of the food on the table and Megan had learned all of their names. The boy was George, and the girls were Susan, Rebecca, and Jean. Rebecca and Jean were first cousins, as were George and Susan, and all were here because their parents had felt this was an opportunity they couldn't pass up.

"My dad, he was a little suspicious," Jean told Megan, "but Momma says nobody don't get too much education."

Rebecca chimed in. "Yes, and my ma says you can trust what Sheriff McCray says and he says you're a good teacher."

"Hey." George pointed to a side window. "Speaking of Sheriff McCray, here he comes now."

A second later, after a perfunctory knock on the kitchen door, Daniel stepped into the breakfast room. "I thought I heard talking back here." He nodded at the four children. "Why didn't you kids wait for me at the station? I thought that's what we agreed to do."

Susan glared at her cousin. "George said there wasn't no need to wait seeing as we knew where to come anyhow."

George shrugged his skinny shoulders. "No harm done I don't reckon. I was hungry and Miss Megan fed us."

Megan looked at Daniel, who appeared as exhausted as she felt. She decided he must have had trouble sleeping too, especially when he stifled a yawn before answering George.

"I'm glad you got something to eat, but Miss Megan isn't supposed to start teaching for another hour. Tomorrow morning if you're hungry, come by the station at eight o'clock and I'll take all of you to the diner for breakfast."

George grinned widely. "Oh boy! I'm glad now that Ma made me come to this extra schooling."

Daniel grinned too. "It's a date then. I'll see you tomorrow morning. Now let's step out on the porch so Miss Megan can finish her coffee and get dressed.

Suddenly aware that she was clad only in her rather short gown and robe, Megan jumped to her feet. "Oh my. Daniel, please watch the children while I dress." She couldn't help noticing the appreciative gleam in his eye when she turned to hurry from the room.

By the end of that week, Megan could measure real progress with all of her students. She felt less sanguine about her relationship with Daniel. Every morning that week he had treated the new students and Mikie to breakfast at the diner and then escorted them to Beth Ann's house where he visited with Megan a few minutes before the tutoring session. Then he found a reason to spend almost every evening with Megan.

Not that she put up a fight. She had decided it would be silly to deny herself the pleasure of Daniel's company when they had so little time remaining together anyway.

And Daniel seemed to feel the same. Every evening he either cooked for Megan and Beth Ann and Trevor, or he wandered across the street and offered to help weed the flower garden or mow the backyard, or whatever needed doing.

On Friday evening, after he had used the excuse

of the upcoming July 4 competition to have them and Mikie over for another cookout, complete with homemade butter pecan ice cream, Megan and Beth Ann were beginning to feel like moochers.

"There's no doubt about it," Megan said that night when she and Beth Ann settled down in the parlor for a chat before going to bed. "We have to have Daniel over for dinner tomorrow evening. I plan to help you in the store again, but we'll have plenty of time if we hurry."

"You're right," Beth Ann said. "What's your specialty?"

Megan grimaced. "I'm a whiz at making toast."

"Great!" Beth Ann slapped a hand to her fore-head in feigned distress. "Just my luck to end up with a cooking partner who can't boil water."

"So what did you expect me to say? That I'd fix the polenta with wild mushrooms and goat cheese while you buttered the rolls?"

Beth Ann chuckled. "If I know Daniel—and I do—he would prefer fried chicken, and I'm pretty good at that. We'll toss in a couple of veggies and you can pick up a cake at Mabel's Bakery and we'll be set."

"Sounds like a plan to me," Megan said, then stifled a yawn. "Guess I'd better turn in. Sounds like we're going to have a busy day tomorrow."

"True. So don't forget to call Daniel tomorrow morning and invite him over."

"Why me?" Megan protested. "It's your house we're inviting him to."

But Beth Ann had already slipped into the hallway and didn't answer.

By 6:00 the following afternoon, Megan and Beth Ann had finished their grocery shopping and lugged their supplies into the kitchen. Megan had dropped by Mabel's Bakery earlier in the day where she'd bought an Italian cream cake, a carrot cake, and a chess pie.

"Good grief," Beth Ann exclaimed when Megan opened the refrigerator to show off her purchases. "Did you invite half the population of the county without telling me?"

"I just wasn't sure what everyone liked."

"Well, I think you've covered all the bases. We'll have to send some dessert home with Daniel or I'll gain ten pounds before Monday."

"Stop complaining," Megan said. "I notice you've bought two kinds of meat. So maybe we really should invite some more people over."

"No way! I'm planning on feeding Trevor leftovers for a week."

Megan slumped against the cabinet. "It's wonderful to think that something worthwhile will come from my exhaustion." She straightened and grinned. "But I'm delighted that we're actually going to pay Daniel back for all the cooking he's done for us lately. Before we get started, I'm going to run upstairs and put on something cooler. Then I'll be back and help you by peeling potatoes or whatever you need me to do."

"Great! What time did you tell Daniel to be here?"

"At eight. That should give us plenty of time, don't you think?"

"Absolutely. So before we get started, I'm going to change into some jeans. I can't fry chicken in this outfit."

"Okay! See you in a few minutes."

An hour later, the potatoes were cooking, the green beans were done and sitting on the warming unit, and Beth Ann was busily flouring the chicken and tenderized steak.

"Okay, I've finished brewing the tea," Megan said. "Shall I take the potato peels out to the compost pile?"

"Listen to you!" Beth Ann rested her flour-covered hands on the edge of a stainless steel bowl and beamed at Megan. "Ten days ago you didn't know what a compost heap was, and today you're talking like a native."

Megan wrinkled her nose. "Oh yes, I've defi-

nitely learned what a compost heap is, and I
could recognize one from the smell at fifty
paces."

"If you weren't such a city girl born and bred,
you'd appreciate that pungent odor."

"Sure, sure," Megan said, pushing the screen
open with her hip. "I'll be back momentarily
and—oops! Ye gads, Daniel, you almost made me
spill the potato peels. What are you doing here?
Dinner isn't for another hour."

Megan looked into Daniel's somber face, then
glanced behind him. "Uncle Dallas! Dad! What on
earth?"

"Dallas?" Beth Ann's gasp was followed by a
clatter of something falling, but Megan was too
unnerved by her visitors to turn and investigate.
"Why are you two here? Is someone ill? Uncle
Dayton? Uncle Denver?"

"Both disgustingly well," Dallas drawled. "I'm
along as escort to your father. We were lucky
enough to find the sheriff in his office, and he
accompanied us here."

Dallas craned his neck and looked into the
kitchen. "A redheaded snow lady," he commented,
and everyone turned to look.

Beth Ann stood over the flour bowl, which rested upside down on the floor. Flour covered the
front of her jeans, and her dark green shirt was
streaked with white dust, as was her face. She held

her flour-covered hands in front of her, still clutching a raw chicken breast, and stared with widened eyes toward her unexpected guests.

Megan's father spoke for the first time. "Megan, dear, I need to talk to you."

Megan nodded. "In a bit," she said, then hurried over to Beth Ann's side. Megan knew her friend had been attracted to her uncle, and she could only imagine Beth Ann's embarrassment. "I'll finish flouring the chicken," Megan whispered. "You go change clothes."

Beth Ann needed no urging. She thrust the chicken breast into Megan's hands and fled.

Megan glanced down at the overturned flour bowl, then at the piece of chicken she held, and finally at Daniel. He gave her a reassuring smile and stepped forward.

"Let me help," he said. He motioned for the other two men to pull up seats at the kitchen table, lowered the heat under Beth Ann's chicken frier, and then picked up the flour bowl and set it to one side. "Where's Trevor?"

"He's in the parlor watching TV," Megan answered.

Daniel looked toward Dallas. "Go find Beth Ann's son in the parlor and tell him he's needed in the kitchen. Through that door, down the hall to your right, third door on the right."

Dallas raised his brows, but he also stood and followed orders without saying a word.

Ten minutes later, Daniel and Trevor had finished sweeping up the flour. Then Daniel found the flour canister and poured some into a fresh bowl. "I'll finish frying the chicken if you'll set extra places in the dining room," he told Megan.

"We can't stay for dinner," Megan's father protested.

"Sure we can," Dallas said. Megan had noticed him occasionally glancing toward the door through which Beth Ann had made her exit.

"You certainly can," Megan chimed in. "We have enough food to feed half the county anyway. We were going to cook a special meal as a treat for Daniel, and here he is cooking for us again."

"My pleasure," Daniel said, smiling at Megan and causing her silly heart to leap.

Five minutes later Beth Ann came back into the kitchen, and Megan smiled to herself. Beth Ann had obviously visited Megan's closet because she now wore one of the sundresses Megan had packed when she left Atlanta. The soft aqua fabric highlighted Beth Ann's porcelain complexion and clung to her curves in ways that had probably never been imagined by its creator. Megan glanced toward Dallas and saw him gulp, but it was her father who jumped to his feet and went to meet Beth Ann.

"Mrs. Stanfield," he said, smiling. "The sheriff told me you've let Megan stay with you during her time in Barbourville. I can't begin to tell you how much I appreciate your kindness."

Megan watched her father charm Beth Ann while Dallas sat alone glowering. She gave a mental shrug. Beth Ann and Dallas were as unsuited to each other as she and Daniel were, so it was no doubt best if their mutual attraction died a natural death.

"Dinner's ready," Daniel announced a few seconds later, and they all trooped into the dining room.

An hour later, after everyone had enjoyed the meal of creamed potatoes, green beans, fried chicken, chicken fried steak, and either pie or cake, Megan finally allowed her father to claim her attention.

"You know we need to talk, Megan," he said to her across the table. "I had thought to speak to you alone, but I can see that you've made some close friends here so I have no qualms about talking in front of them. Your Uncle Dallas came to Atlanta to tell me you're looking for a job and housing in Chicago, and I realized that I've been wrong in trying to deny you your dream in order to protect you. I want you to come back to Atlanta. Not only will I refrain from standing in your way, but I'll also help you. In fact, I've set up an appointment for you to interview with the school system on Wednesday of next week."

Megan knew just how difficult it had been for her father to speak those words, and she didn't want to disappoint him, but she shook her head. "I'm sorry, Dad, but I have commitments that will keep me here for another three weeks. After that, I'll be glad to interview."

Her father grimaced. "Wednesday is the last day to interview for the coming school year. Understandably, they need to get everything lined up as soon as possible."

"Then I'll just have to wait. I can't leave McCray County yet."

"Yes you can," Daniel said.

Startled, Megan jerked her head around to look at him. "What do you mean? You know I can't leave the children in mid-session."

"Yes you can," Daniel repeated. "They'll understand that you've been called away by circumstances beyond your control. You don't want to put this interview off for another year."

"Daniel's right," her father said. "You say this is what you've always wanted to do, so now is the time to begin."

Megan pushed herself to her feet and looked around the table. Beth Ann and Trevor stared at her with sad smiles, but both nodded their agreement with her father. Dallas looked down into his empty plate, neither agreeing nor disagreeing, and Daniel watched her with thinned lips and squared shoulders. He had already made his opinion crystal clear: He wanted her to go.

"Very well," Megan said, aware that her stomach was sinking toward her toes. "I'll wind up my tutoring session on Monday and drive back to Atlanta on Tuesday."

Chapter Thirteen

By 1:00 on Tuesday afternoon, when Daniel helped her fit her last piece of luggage into the trunk of her car, Megan was wrung out emotionally.

She had just spent two days saying good-bye to people she had come to love in a very short period of time. Judge McCray had taken her hand and smiled sadly, telling her he was going to miss her. Neither mentioned that she was a week shy of her four weeks of community service, and Megan could only assume that Daniel had filled in his uncle about her situation.

The disappointment of her students at Monday morning's tutoring session had almost reduced her to tears, but she had promised to come back and

175

visit again soon, a promise she fully intended to keep.

After all, there was no way she was going to lose touch with Beth Ann and Trevor. Beth Ann was the closest friend Megan had ever known, and Trevor was a dear boy she hoped to watch grow up to be a fine young man.

But Daniel was undoubtedly the most difficult for her to leave. She knew now that she loved him deeply and unconditionally, and if he had asked her to stay, she would have tossed her dream aside in order to be with him.

But he continued to encourage her to go even though, whenever she caught him looking at her when he didn't think she'd notice, the expression in his eyes was so sad she was hard pressed not to fling herself into his arms and swear she'd never leave him.

But she couldn't help wondering if he'd welcome her undying love, even if she had the courage to offer it. He was careful not to touch her any time they were together on Sunday, and on Monday morning when he escorted the children to the parlor for the last time.

And so she tried not to touch him either, aware that to do so might make it even harder for her to leave. She almost regretted that he had to be there for her departure by virtue of the fact that he had papers for her to sign before she took possession of her car again.

He had arrived at the last possible minute, just seconds before the hour when they had decided she would go. Beth Ann and Trevor were there, but they stayed in the background, having said their good-byes before Daniel arrived with the car.

"I'll load those," he had said, nodding toward her luggage stacked on the sidewalk. In addition to the suitcase she had come with, Megan had shopping bags full of clothes she had bought from Beth Ann, not to mention the hummingbird feeder Trevor had made for her from a two-liter soda bottle.

Megan nodded and stepped back, wishing this was over, wishing she didn't have to say good-bye. She watched Daniel place her belongings in her trunk and hoped she would always remember the line of his jaw, the sound of his voice, the twinkle that sometimes brightened his eyes.

"Your luggage is loaded," he said, slamming the trunk lid. "Have you signed the release form?"

Megan handed the form to him. "Tell the Stubblefield brothers I appreciate their taking such good care of the car."

"I'll tell them." He stepped around the car and opened the driver's side door. "Are you ready to go?"

Megan longed to walk into his arms and kiss him until they were both dizzy but his gaze was distant and his lips thinned. And so she merely nodded and stepped around the car, pausing to wave to Beth Ann and Trevor standing on the front porch steps.

"Thanks for everything," she said, slipping into the driver's seat.

"Drive careful." He closed the door and walked away.

Megan turned the key in the ignition and listened to the engine purr to life. With a final wave to the two on the steps, she pulled away from the curb and drove off.

Fifteen minutes later, Megan was on Highway 152, headed out of McCray County. The air was fresh and relatively cool, but she decided not to roll down her window, recalling the bee that had flown in the last time she had been rounding these curves.

Instead, she turned on her air conditioner but slowed down to glance at the scenery. Wild rhododendron still bloomed sporadically along the highway, and a few wildflowers she didn't recognize brought color to the shoulder of the road.

She loved this country, she realized. Its lush greenery, its bright blue skies, its untamed growth of native flowers. And she loved Daniel McCray and she loved McCray County and she loved the children she was leaving behind.

"Dear heavens," she murmured to herself. "What am I doing? I'm leaving behind the life I want in order to pursue a dream that's no longer mine."

Rural children, she realized, were not that much different than the children of urban life. Their life experiences might differ but their needs for a caring, nurturing teacher did not, and she had discovered an affinity within herself for rural children she would not have dreamed was possible.

If she went back, she could fill out the paperwork for certification in Tennessee, then apply for a teaching position in McCray County for the coming fall. She wanted that, she realized, even if Daniel decided he couldn't settle for a socialite who wasn't a native of McCray County.

Immediately, she began watching for a place where she could turn around, but she drove another two miles before she spotted a wide shoulder. She quickly braked, pulled off, looked in both directions, and then pulled across the highway and headed back north. Seconds later she saw blue lights in her rearview mirror.

She sighed, pulled to the shoulder of the road, and rolled down her window.

"Illegal U-turn," Horace commented, strolling up to her car window. "I'm going to have to take you in. Follow me to the station."

"Now just a minute, Deputy Barnhart," Megan

said, thrusting her head out her window and yelling at his retreating back.

"You can talk in the station," Horace called back over his shoulder. "Follow me."

"I can't believe this," Megan grumbled to herself fifteen minutes later when she turned into the parking lot of the McCray County sheriff's office. "Horace has gone too far this time. I'm going to sue . . ."

Horace stepped to the side of her car and opened the door. "Inside," he commanded.

Megan climbed out and marched ahead of Horace to the door of the station. She jerked it open and stepped inside.

Daniel stood beside his desk. A large box sat on the chair that had once attached itself to Megan's rump, and Daniel was placing folders into it. "What are you doing here?" he demanded.

"Horace, of course," Megan ground out through clenched teeth. "He's accusing me of an illegal U-turn."

"Then where is he?" Daniel asked, a frown of confusion touching his forehead.

"Well, right—" Megan turned around in time to see Horace's car pulling out of the parking lot.

"I'll be! He couldn't let me come back on my own, could he?"

"You were coming back?"

"Yes."

"What for? Did you forget something?"

"No, actually I found something."

"What?"

"A new dream. I want to teach in McCray County, and I'm hoping I can get the sheriff to put in a good word for me. I hear he has connections." Megan smiled before walking up to Daniel and wrapping her arms around his waist.

He pulled her into a bear hug, kissed her, and then demanded, "Are you sure?"

"Absolutely." She glanced down at the chair and saw that Daniel had dropped the name plate from his desk into the box sitting there. "What are you doing?"

"Packing. I've resigned as sheriff of McCray County."

"What? But why?"

"So I could apply for a job in Atlanta, of course. I couldn't let you give up your dream, but I couldn't live without you either."

"Oh, Daniel!" Megan felt tears burning at the back of her eyes. "You couldn't be happy living outside McCray County."

"My love, I could be happy living anywhere with you. Will you marry me?"

"Yes, yes, yes." Megan hugged him closer, then lifted her face for another kiss.

The bell above the door jingled and they jumped apart.

"Well, well," Judge McCray said, grinning at Megan and Daniel. "Horace told me I should get over here. Looks like he was right. Danny boy, I've brought your badge to give back to you. I can't accept your resignation after all."

"Okay," Daniel said. "I agree to take it back. Now will you go away?"

"Not until you say I can officiate at your wedding."

"I think the bride should make that decision, Uncle Bob."

"The prisoner, you mean?"

Megan laughed. "Yes, Judge McCray, you can officiate at my wedding. After all, considering that I'm a prisoner of love, I'd probably better have the county judge on my side."

"Well said, Miz Marsh. And I'm sure my dear Evelyn would love to help you with all of the . . ."

The judge paused, then shut his mouth. Neither of the parties that made up his audience was paying the least bit of attention to him.

But he chuckled as he sauntered toward the door. "Just as I predicted," he murmured softly, rubbing his hands together. "A life sentence, and she couldn't be happier."